There he was

Olivia froze, and then her heart took off in an out-of-control gallop. Any semblance of poise she might have gained in her years as a professional broadcaster completely deserted her. She stood in front of him as vulnerable as if she was seventeen again and head over heels in love.

To say he looked good would have been an understatement.

"Olivia."

Olivia. Not Liv as she had once been to him. The greeting was arctic cold, his whole demeanor one of stiff politeness.

"Hello, John."

"Mind if I ask what you're doing here?"

People were staring. She felt their curious gazes and heard the whispers. She willed her voice toward something close to indifference when she said, "The same thing as everyone else in our class."

"Everyone else is welcome here."

Dear Reader,

I've always loved a good reunion story. I like to believe that certain people really are meant to be together, and that even when life throws them some pretty hefty obstacles, they still find their way back to each other. Such is John and Olivia's story.

There are a lot of ways to define success in the careers we've chosen. For me, it's the letter I receive from a reader who thought about my story long enough after closing the book to write and tell me so. With so many outlets to turn to for entertainment in our increasingly high-tech world, I think we readers share a special understanding of what it is to open a book and spend a few hours engrossed in the lives of characters we grow to love. I really hope you'll enjoy following John and Olivia to their fifteen-year high school reunion and meeting their old friends Cleeve and Lori.

I would love to hear from you! My e-mail address is inglathc@aol.com, or write to me at P.O. Box 973, Rocky Mount, VA 24151.

All best,

Inglath

John Riley's Girl

Inglath Cooper

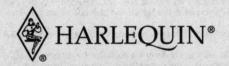

HARLEQUIN®

TORONTO • NEW YORK • LONDON
AMSTERDAM • PARIS • SYDNEY • HAMBURG
STOCKHOLM • ATHENS • TOKYO • MILAN • MADRID
PRAGUE • WARSAW • BUDAPEST • AUCKLAND

ISBN 0-373-71198-0

JOHN RILEY'S GIRL

Copyright © 2004 by Inglath Cooper.

For my Lori. Who would have thought, all those years ago,
we would still be best friends?

And for Mac. Again, for believing.

Books by Inglath Cooper

HARLEQUIN SINGLE TITLE
728—THE LAST GOOD MAN
1174—A WOMAN LIKE ANNIE

Don't miss any of our special offers. Write to us at the
following address for information on our newest releases.

Harlequin Reader Service
U.S.: 3010 Walden Ave., P.O. Box 1325, Buffalo, NY 14269
Canadian: P.O. Box 609, Fort Erie, Ont. L2A 5X3

CHAPTER ONE

The Invitation

"AND THAT'S YOUR update for this Friday evening, May 23. I'm Olivia Ashford sitting in for Robert Marshall."

Olivia held her smile, a smile reflecting cool assurance that she was there to report the truth and nothing but. The cameraman directly in front of her signaled they were off the air and gave her a thumbs-up.

"Good job, Olivia," he said.

A chorus of agreement from the rest of the crew followed the compliment.

"Robert better get back from that island soon, or he might not have a job waiting for him!" Mandy Overstreet was a young assistant producer whose smile held the same wattage as her red hair. Unlike Olivia's, it did not reflect the polish of practice so much as spontaneity. But then she was still in the early throes of infatuation with broadcasting. Olivia had been, too, early on. Before she'd learned that *expendable* was a word that loomed on her career horizon with a billboard that read: Mess Up and There's Always Someone to Replace You.

"Thanks, everybody. You guys make it easy." Olivia unhooked her microphone and got up from behind the desk.

"Nicely done." Michael O'Roarke stood a few feet from the anchor platform, his arms folded across his chest, his blue gaze warm.

"Thanks." Olivia unbuttoned her suit jacket and loosened the collar of her blouse.

They wound their way through a maze of desks to the long corridor that led to Olivia's office. "Hey, we like you up there in the top spot," Art, a senior writer for the evening news, boomed out in a Boston baritone.

"Thanks, Art. Your words, though."

He grinned. "You make 'em sound good."

Inside Olivia's office, Michael closed the door behind them. Olivia had intended to change the formal mahogany furniture in which someone else had dressed the room, but she had never gotten around to moving it to the top of the to-do list. And so she'd left it, feeling the ill fit of it, as if she were borrowing someone else's clothes. Sometimes, her whole life felt like that, as if it didn't really belong to her.

"It's yours, you know. That job is yours." Michael sliced a hand through the air, a smile cracking his face wide open.

"Isn't that jumping the gun a bit?" Olivia laughed, raising an eyebrow. "This was my first night sitting in for him."

"But Robert's going to retire. Everyone knows it. You've been on the morning show for almost three years. And I'm sorry, but people are going to like your beautiful blue-eyed self in a spot where they're used to seeing a stiff."

"Michael—"

"I know. You don't like to talk about things before they happen. But I don't think you can jinx this one. It's just about as sure a thing as sure gets."

"There's nothing sure or predictable in this business," Olivia disagreed, even though it was clear she was at least being considered for the position. Who would have thought the nearly destitute young girl who'd answered an ad in a newspaper for the job of receptionist would ever end up here?

It had been a long climb.

Michael tilted his head in reluctant agreement. "Granted. But I think it's going to be yours if you want it."

Olivia rubbed the back of her neck where tension had unfolded and now blanketed her shoulders with clamplike intensity.

"Here, let me." Michael stepped forward to knead the knotted muscles, his touch efficient. "Wow, you *are* tense."

"You should do this for a living."

"Michael O'Roarke. Personal masseur," he teased.

"You'd miss the power lunches."

"Ouch. But yeah, probably so."

As the morning show's executive producer, Michael had hired Olivia three years ago as a fill-in anchor. She'd eventually become full-time. The two of them had tried a route other than friendship in the beginning. But a week skiing in Aspen had given them both a reality check. Seven straight days together had etched a convincing enough picture of why permanent wasn't in the cards for them.

It had taken them both a good six months to admit it wasn't going to work. But miraculously, they'd survived as friends. Good friends, really. And that was something she didn't take for granted.

Before Michael, she'd kept her life bare of serious relationships. There had been a couple of forays toward something more than casual dating, but there was always a reason to nip it in the bud. The guys were too assertive, too passive, too tall, too short, too aloof, too needy. Too something.

From this, she had developed a reputation for being career-driven in each of the stations where she'd worked. She'd heard the labels attached to her name by some of the men whose interest she had not indulged: ice princess, Miss North Pole. None of them exactly original, and there had been a few that didn't get anywhere near that flattering. But the reputation suited Olivia. As did being alone. At least until recently.

Recently, the void in her life seemed to yawn wider with every achievement and every year that went by. She had once thought success, like ordinary old spackle, would fill the holes, heal any residual wounds and declare to the world that she was a person who had something to offer. But sometimes, mostly at night, she would wonder: Am I going to be alone for the rest of my life? Is that what I want? Isn't there anything more than this?

In the light of day, the panic resumed its day job as logic, and her own answer to the question was that a person could not expect to have everything. She had made work the emphasis in her life, and for the most part, it was a good life.

The phone buzzed. She stepped away from Michael's attentive hands and picked up the receiver. "Yes, Daphne?"

"There's a woman on line three who says she went to high school with you. A Lori Morgan Peters? Want me to take a message?"

Olivia blinked. Her lips parted, then pressed together. Lori?

"You still there?"

"Ah, yes. Thanks, Daphne. I'll take it." To Michael, she murmured, "Excuse me," then circumnavigated the desk and sat down in her chair.

He hooked a thumb toward the doorway. "See you in the morning."

She nodded, exhaling hard. Lori. It had been fifteen years since they'd graduated from high school, since Olivia had left the town where they'd both grown up, without ever saying goodbye. Sheer cowardice nearly made her buzz Daphne back and ask for that message. But an inner voice taunted. *Come on, Olivia, be an adult. The past is a lot of miles behind you.* She drew in a deep breath and pushed the blinking light on her phone. "Lori?"

"Olivia? I can't believe I actually got through to you!"

The voice, laced with shock, sent her reeling back a decade and a half, to another place, another life. "Goodness. What a wonderful surprise. How are you?"

"Fine, fine." Her one-time best friend laughed. "And I don't have to ask how you are. Obviously, great!"

The assertion carried not an ounce of resentment. But then that was the Lori she remembered. Olivia pictured her as she'd been during their high-school years. Barely five feet tall. Sky-blue eyes. Freckles scattered across her nose. A petite-framed girl with an unerring belief in herself and the possibilities available in the world around her. "Things are pretty good," she said.

"We keep up with you around here, you know.

The town library even has a whole section devoted to your career.''

Olivia knew this, of course. The Lanford County Library had contacted her a number of times, asking if she would be willing to address some of the high-school students interested in journalism, but she had never accepted the invitation. Doing so would have meant going back to Summerville, and after that one last time, it had never again been a consideration.

Olivia gripped the receiver. ''Where are you? What are you doing these days?''

''In Summerville. After college, I worked as a chemist for a pharmaceutical company. Then I met the love of my life, moved back and now have four children. Dorothy was right. There's no place like home.''

Home. By all rights, Summerville wasn't really home to her. She had no family there anymore. No ties. Other than memories, of course. But while a person could pack her bags and leave a place behind for good, the same could not be said of memories. Memory had tentacles. ''Your family. They're all okay, I hope?''

''I lost my dad a few years ago,'' Lori said, her voice softening.

''Oh, Lori.'' Olivia's hand flew to her chest. ''I'm sorry.''

''Thanks.''

Olivia didn't miss the catch in her old friend's

voice. She remembered spending nights at Lori's house, a big white pre–Civil War farmhouse that had been in her family for generations. It had a fireplace in every bedroom, an amazing thing to Olivia who'd never imagined houses having such things. It was the kind of house that always smelled as though there were oatmeal cookies baking in the oven. And she remembered envying the closeness of that family. How they had all so obviously loved one another despite the typical arguments between brothers and sisters, which Lori's round, cherry-cheeked mother had refereed with good humor. In many ways, it had seemed like heaven on earth to Olivia. So different from her own home.

"Mom's fine, though," Lori went on. "And Sally-Anne, you remember my youngest sister, she's pregnant for the first time, big as a small elephant, and making us all pay for the fact that we said the family needed another grandchild." An affectionate chuckle followed the assertion, setting off another unwelcome hollow echo inside Olivia.

"No, life's pretty normal around here. Not too exciting the way your life must be. Interviewing celebrities every day. Sitting on the same couch as that gorgeous Derek Phillips." She drew *gorgeous* out to three syllables. "I bet you can't wait to get out of bed every morning. I know I wouldn't be able to."

The awe in Lori's voice was something Olivia had

grown used to hearing in the voices of strangers
since she had become a public figure. But hearing
it in her old friend's voice felt off-key.

"So did you get the invitation?" Lori asked.

"Invitation?"

"To our high-school reunion."

Surprise zinged through Olivia. Reunion. "No. I
didn't."

"Oh, no," Lori said, her voice devoid of its former buoyancy. "I was certain it would have gotten
there by now. I was just calling to make sure. I sort
of got lassoed into organizing the thing."

Olivia glanced at the stack of mail in the center
of her desk—three days worth. "It could be here. I
have a bunch of mail I haven't opened yet."

"Well, anyway, it's on the fifth of June. Is there
any way you could come? It'd be so great to see
you."

"It would be wonderful to see you, too, but I
don't think I could possibly get away," Olivia said
quickly, not giving herself a chance to consider doing anything else. There had been times, through the
years, when the yearning to go back to Summerville
had throbbed like an old injury that makes itself
known on rainy days. She had not indulged the
throbbing, intense as it had become at times. Her
old life in Summerville was over.

"I should have called you sooner," Lori said, disappointment edging the words. "But actually,

everyone else thought you'd be too busy to come. With your schedule and everything, I mean. I thought there might be a slight chance.''

Olivia felt somehow small and disloyal for proving Lori wrong and the rest of them right.

"I'm sorry," she said, even as a little voice screamed in her ear: *Don't be a coward, Olivia! You could go!* But logic asserted itself as well, and there was too much old pain there, too many memories better left in place.

"Oh."

A dozen questions weighted the one-word response. Her friend from long ago would have asked them. *Why did you leave? Why haven't you ever come back?* Olivia felt tangible distance between them now, and part of her rebelled. Lori had once been her best friend, and hearing her voice for the first time in so many years stirred up fresh regret for letting something so meaningful slip away.

"I'd really love to see you, Lori. Maybe you could come to D.C. and visit sometime?"

A pause and then, "Well, sure."

The words sounded empty, and too polite. Not the kind of words you said to someone you'd once saved a seat for on the school bus every day, shared lockers with, written notes back and forth to during Mr. Primrose's study hall. "Really, let's plan a weekend sometime soon."

"I might just take you up on it," Lori said, her voice brightening a little.

"I hope you will."

Silence gripped them then. How could awkwardness manage such a stranglehold on two people who had once been so close?

"Well, I know you must be busy, Olivia. It was good to talk to you. If you change your mind, here's my number." She reeled it off while Olivia scribbled it on the notepad in front of her, vowing to call and invite Lori for a visit just as soon as things slowed down a bit and ignoring the voice that said they never did. Or she never let them.

"We'll talk soon, okay?"

"Sure, Olivia. Take care."

They said goodbye and hung up. Olivia's hand lingered on the receiver, some part of her reluctant to break the connection. She was overcome by a sudden urge to call Lori back and tell her she would come. She missed their friendship with a keen sense of longing and loss.

Olivia let go after a few regretful moments, then reached across the desk and picked up the pile of mail. Sifting through the stack, she singled out an envelope, turned it over and looked at the return address on the back seal.

Summerville, Virginia.

Her heart dropped, even though over the years, she had received what amounted to boxes of mail with postmarks from her former hometown. But her reaction was always the same. Her hope, unwelcome though it was, always the same.

Daphne had already slit open the envelope. Olivia slipped out the heavy card inside.

Hard to believe, but yes,
we are old enough to have a 15-year class reunion! (Yikes!!)
Are you brave enough to attend?
We hope so!
What: A weekend of reuniting!
Events taking place Thursday through Saturday.
Where: Lanford County Community Center
When: June 5-7
Why? Because that's the only way you'll get to see how we all turned out!

She dropped the card onto the desk, overcome with a wave of nostalgia for some precious things she had lost long ago. She swiveled her chair away from the desk and settled her gaze on the D.C. skyline outside her office window. So many buildings. So many people. In comparison, Summerville was another world altogether. Had it changed? Were the people there any different than they'd been fifteen years ago? Was the dilapidated old house she'd grown up in still standing? Was the farmer's market still held downtown every Saturday morning rain or shine? Was John still there?

With the name a memory came floating up and emotion knotted in her throat. Lori working the summer of their junior year at the Just-a-Minute Drive-In. Olivia and John parked out front in his battered old Dodge pickup boasting four different layers of paint. He'd bought it himself with money he'd saved working summers on his dad's farm, and he couldn't have been more proud of it had it been bought right off the assembly line. Olivia sitting in the middle of the seat, her shoulder tucked under his arm. Lori ducking inside the rolled-down window and telling them not to order any fries because Cecil Callaway had just dropped a fly in the deep fryer.

She could still hear John's laughter, the deep, full rumble that had never failed to warm her, fill her with something satisfying and secure. She had loved to hear him laugh, had taken delight in being the one to make him do so. And as strange as it would have sounded to anyone else, considering that nearly every cheerleader at Summerville High would have given up her spot on the squad for a date with John Riley, it was his laughter that had drawn her to him when he'd asked her out at the beginning of their junior year.

There had been so little laughter in her own house. Her father had long before convinced himself he had nothing to laugh about. And Olivia had learned early on to censor hers if she wanted to avoid the frown of disapproval that always followed.

To her, John's laughter had held the power of a healing touch, made her feel that everything would be all right. She'd been wrong about that part. Laughter didn't fix anything; it just made things a little more bearable.

She could have asked Lori about him. Wished now with an ache that she had. But then what good would it have done? John had made another life for himself, moved on to someone else.

Olivia picked up the card, read it again, then stuck it back in the envelope. She thought of the possibilities in her immediate future—a chance at the main anchor position for her network, a position someone starting out in broadcasting could only dream of.

This was a good change, the kind that should fill a person with satisfaction and a feeling of success.

She got up from her desk, went to the window that took up nearly one side of the corner office and looked down at the traffic below.

With all that, why then this feeling of rootlessness, as if her entire existence were only surface-deep and the slightest unbalancing would topple her over into nothingness? Why was it that she lived her life like someone afraid that a snap of the fingers would make it all suddenly disappear?

There was something about hearing Lori's disappointment that made her wonder: Why can't I go back?

It would be so great to see you.

Why not?

For so long, she had avoided too much thought of the place where she'd grown up, the people she had known there. She'd ignored it, as if in doing so the memories would eventually disappear altogether.

But life didn't really work that way, did it? Wasn't it only in facing up to those things with the power to haunt that a person ever stood a chance of overcoming them?

And Olivia had never done that.

She'd just walked away, closed the door.

Fifteen years ago, she had needed to cut all ties to her home. To maintain even one would have been to remain piped into things too painful for her to hear. And so she had shoved her entire life there into a box that she'd sealed up and vowed never to open.

But Lori's call had brought front and center recognition of exactly how much she had lost fifteen years ago. Not just John and the future they had planned together. But so many other things, as well. A friendship whose equal she had never again found. And the simple right to revisit the place where she had grown up. Rocky as that childhood had been, it was hers.

Standing here above a city where she had never

felt as if she really fitted, Olivia wondered if maybe it was time to go home. Maybe it wasn't too late to reclaim some of the past—own up to it and then put it away for good. This time with peace and acceptance.

Was she strong enough to do that and walk away again?

There was only one way to find out.

CHAPTER TWO

Should Have Said No

HE DESERVED a good swift kick in the pants.

Any man who let his home be turned into a three-ring circus for a weekend deserved nothing less.

From the door of the brood mare barn, John Riley watched the half-dozen workers in his front yard hammering tent stakes into the ground, transforming the state's biggest cutting-horse farm into the stage for his fifteen-year class reunion.

When a water pipe had burst at the Community Center earlier that morning, flooding the place and rendering it unusable, Lori Peters had called John in a panic, vowing indebtedness to him for life if he would agree to have the weekend-long reunion at Rolling Hills. In the face of her desperation—*Please, John, I'll never ask you for another favor as long as I live. The park is already booked this weekend, and there's nowhere else we can rent last-minute big enough for all these tents*—there weren't many excuses he could have made without sounding like a selfish jerk. So here he stood, cursing the decision that ensured there was no earthly way he could get out of going to the thing now.

On a normal day, Rolling Hills Farm was not an inactive place. In the summer heat, horses were worked early, starting at 6:00 a.m. There was usually a tractor or two running somewhere within earshot, a cow calling for its calf, a mare nickering for her foal. But the reunion being staged on his front lawn had turned it into nothing short of chaos.

Given the choice, he'd gladly snap his fingers and make it all disappear, the Great Party Setup's cotton-candy-pink van and all.

Across the yard stood a man in overalls, a sleeveless T-shirt and a tattoo of a rooster on his left arm. He hammered a tent stake into the ground, straightened and, without missing a beat, sent a stream of tobacco juice arcing over his right shoulder. It landed on a cluster of snow-white azaleas encircling the base of an old oak tree.

Anger launched John straight across the stretch of grass between the barn and the house where he lit into the man like fire on October leaves.

"Those were my wife's flowers you just spit on," he said, the words curt.

The man wiped the back of his hand across the tobacco leak at the corner of his mouth. "Hey, bud, I'm really sorry."

"Next time maybe you could have a little more courtesy for where you're aiming."

"No problem." The man grabbed his tools and trotted back to his truck, lobbing worried glances over his shoulder as he went.

John snatched the hose from the side of the house, turned on the faucet and rinsed every speck of tobacco juice from the flowers, turning them white again.

He looked down the hill at the farm spread out below with its bright spots of color. After Laura had found out she was sick, she had begun planting things everywhere. Pear trees, peach trees, boxwoods. Her favorite had been the white azaleas. She had never said it, and John would never have put his thoughts into words, but he knew it had been her way of leaving something of herself behind. When he had first realized what she was doing, he couldn't look at her without going off by himself and crying in impotent rage. He had never let her see him. And it was now one of his greatest regrets. He'd wanted to be strong for her, to pretend that everything was going to be all right, when they both knew that it wasn't. He wished now that he'd let her see his sadness. He'd tried to do what he thought was the right thing for her. It was only after she died, unexpectedly one night, that he realized she would never know how great his loss had been.

And for that he couldn't forgive himself.

Looking back on it, he'd thought going on with their lives was the right thing to do. If they saw the doctors, underwent the treatments, then she would get well. Wasn't that how it was supposed to work? Part of that had to be *believing* she would get well. If they talked about the possibility that she might die, then it might happen.

And it had.

He hung the hose up, stomped back across the yard to the white-and-green barn where Hank Owens stood in the middle of the big sliding doors, arms folded across his chest, a frown on his weathered face.

"I know I'm a jackass, Hank. I don't need you to tell me again."

Hank stopped him at the door with a gloved hand. "I don't blame you for tearing into his butt. I saw how hard she worked on those darn flowers."

A mixture of approval and disapproval laced his voice, deep and resonant, like a Baptist preacher's at a revival. To most of the world, Hank was an intimidating man. He had shoulders wider than a stall door, hands callused from decades of hard work, legs slightly bowed from a lifetime of sitting on a horse. He had been at Rolling Hills longer than John had been alive, and John had no illusions about who was the glue that had held the place together in the first few months after Laura had died.

"It's been almost two years, John." Compassion

softened the rough edge of Hank's voice. "Maybe you oughta talk to somebody about this. Somebody impartial."

"So they can tell me how it's normal to be angry because my wife died long before I figured out how to make her happy?"

Hank shook his head and managed to look more worried. "She was happy, John."

"Not the way she could have been if I—"

"If you'd what?"

"Nothing," he said, putting brakes on the conversation. Talking about it didn't do any good, anyway. He couldn't change any of it—couldn't go back and make himself a better husband. No matter how much he might wish for the chance.

"You gotta get a handle on this, son. Somehow. Someway." Hank's words were low and insistent. "If not for anybody else, then for her." He tipped his gaze toward the road at the foot of the driveway where a school bus had just slowed to a halt.

The stop sign popped out from the side, warning lights flashing. The door opened, and out bounded Flora, pigtails bobbing, her Black Beauty lunch box in one hand, a Barbie backpack slung over her other shoulder.

She looked both ways before crossing the road, just as John had taught her. His heart swelled. She walked until she reached the gates to the farm, but as soon as her sneakers left the main road, she was off and running, up the long driveway to the house.

In the months after Laura had died, he had insisted on picking Flora up from school every day, but she had wanted to ride the bus and had finally told him so. "Daddy, I'll come back. I won't leave like Mommy did. I promise." Her intuition had been entirely too accurate for a seven-year-old. Enough so that he had given in and made it a daily struggle not to let her sense his irrational fear that he would somehow lose her, too.

She was skipping now, zigzagging back and forth on the hardtop driveway. Halfway up, she stopped and picked a cluster of yellow buttercups, which he knew would be for Sophia.

He waited where he was, raising a hand in greeting when she looked toward the barn and caught sight of Hank and him. She made an all-out sprint across the grass then, the smile on her face putting that now-predictable squeeze on his heart. The strength of I'll-do-anything-for-you love was something he had never understood until he experienced it firsthand.

"Daddy!" Her voice was strong and clear, and it carried across the wide expanse of lawn that stretched between the house and the brood-mare barn.

"Hey, sweet pea. Looks like you could just about outrun Naddie today."

The sound of his daughter's laughter was the only thing capable of thawing the coldness Laura's death had left inside him. Flora loved nothing more than being compared to Nadine, the two-and-a-half-year-old filly who was all but guaranteed to become cutting-horse royalty.

Nadine's entrance into the world had been anything but easy. They had nearly lost her, and once her spindly legs had found their way to the ground, the mare had rejected her. By all logic, the foal should have died. But she had more than her share of fight in her. John had his own belief about the connection between the young horse and his daughter. From the first moment Flora had stuck her hand through the rails of the foal's stall, a bond had formed. Flora had witnessed her own mother's extraordinary will to live, and John could only think that on some level, she and the young filly both understood what it was to fight for life and refuse to let go.

Ten feet from the barn door, Flora dropped her backpack and lunch box, and whirled at John like a tiny tornado, launching herself into his arms.

"Whoa there, little pony."

She giggled again, locking her arms around his neck. Sweet emotion flooded through him. Love. Pure, simple, undiluted, unconditional. There were no strings attached, no "I'll-love-you-forever-ifs." It simply was.

"Are we having a circus, Daddy?"

"All but," John said, ignoring Hank's look of disapproval. "No, honey, those tents are for a class reunion."

"What's a reunion?"

"It's when a bunch of people get together and talk about things that don't matter anymore."

"Oh. If it doesn't matter, then why are you having it?"

"Because sometimes grown-ups have to do things they'd rather not do."

"Why?"

"Because they're grown-ups."

More head shaking from Hank.

"Hi, Hank," Flora said from her position in John's arms.

"Hey, itty-bitty." Hank tugged on one of her pigtails. "How was school today?"

"Good. Guess what I did?"

"Something smart, I'll bet."

"I drew a picture of Naddie."

"Can I see it?"

Flora unzipped her book bag, pulled out a piece of green construction paper with an orange horse on it.

"That's a mighty fine likeness," Hank said.

"It sure is," John agreed.

"Can I go see her?"

John set his daughter down. "You know Sophia's got your snack waiting."

"Just for a minute?"

"All right."

She took his hand, then held out the other for Hank, skipping between them down the center aisle of the barn and chattering about her day along the way. He and Hank responded at the appropriate moments, smiles on both their faces. Hank loved her as if she were his own, and John was glad of it. If Laura had taught him anything, it was the value of love. That you could never have too much or give too much. He only wished he'd learned that lesson sooner. It was such an easy thing to give. Or it should be, anyway.

Outside, they crossed another expanse of grass and made their way into the barn where the two-year-olds were kept. A chorus of whinnies announced their entrance.

"I believe Miss Nadine knows you're here," Hank said.

"She always knows, doesn't she, Hank?"

"Yep. She sure does."

Hearing her name, the filly let out another loud whinny from her stall some twenty feet away.

"Just a minute, Naddie." Flora darted into Hank's office and charged back out a couple of seconds later with the filly's customary afternoon carrots.

John and Hank shook their heads. By the time they caught up with her, Flora was already in the stall. The chestnut filly used her soft muzzle to gently poke about Flora's body in a game of find-the-carrot. Flora giggled when Nadine nosed her right pocket and followed it up with a prod at her armpit. The horse reached around then and found what she was looking for, the three carrots sticking out of Flora's back pocket. She let out a soft nicker that clearly meant: "I won—now give them to me."

"Okay, okay." Flora pulled one from her pocket and gave it to the young horse, who took one polite bite at a time, her beautiful head bobbing in enthusiasm.

"She looked pretty good on the lunge line this afternoon," Hank said. "The stiffness in that right leg seems to have worked itself out."

"No bute?"

"Nope."

"Good. Let's baby it a while longer, though."

"Daddy?"

"What, sweet pea?"

"When can I ride Naddie?"

"Right after you start dating."

Hank shook his head again and chuckled.

Flora gave him a look that would no doubt be perfected by the time she actually *did* start dating.

"Someday," he said, refining his answer. "Naddie's still green, honey. Popcorn is exactly what you need right now."

"But Popcorn is slow."

"Slow is good."

A rumble sounded in the sky above the barn. Just as John reached to pull Flora out of the stall, a military jet roared over, so low it sounded as if it had grazed the very top of the barn roof. Nadine snorted, danced sideways, eyes wide, head high.

"There's got to be something we can do to get them to alter their flight path," Hank said as the sound faded. "Somebody's going to get hurt."

John sighed. He'd made a dozen phone calls. All to no avail so far.

The farm lay in the direct path of the drills the jets conducted periodically. There seemed to be no rhyme or reason to their schedule so that they never knew when one would thunder over, so low they could see the pilot if they looked up.

"It's all right, girl," he said now to Nadine. And then to Flora, "Sophia's going to fuss if you don't get those cookies while they're warm. Why don't you go on up to the house now?"

Flora reluctantly said goodbye to Nadine who let out a protesting whinny.

"I'll be back," she promised. "Be good."

"Fat chance," Hank said. "As soon as you get out the barn door, we'll have Miss Prima Donna on our hands again."

Flora giggled. "She's not bad, Hank."

"Oh, just perfectly willing to kick the stall door down if you don't come when she wants you to."

"I'll make some more calls about the jets, Hank," John said over his shoulder as he and Flora headed out of the barn.

"Somebody ought to be able to do something," Hank said.

The cell phone in John's pocket rang. "You go on up, honey. I'll be right behind you."

"Okay, Daddy." She sprinted off across the yard, disappearing through the back door even as he reached for the phone, punched a button and said, "Hello."

"Hey. Hear you're havin' a reunion out there."

John looked down at the grass, gave a renegade dandelion a booted swat. "Hey, Cleeve. Wish I could deny it."

"What'd I tell you about being the nice guy?"

"I'm not feeling too nice these days."

"Well, this oughta at least qualify you for saint-hood or somethin' darn close."

"Somethin'." John smiled, Cleeve's intention, he was sure. Getting John to smile had been one of Cleeve's goals for the better part of the past two years. It wasn't often he succeeded, but Cleeve was a firm believer in humor's ability to heal most of life's gashes. "When'd you get back?"

"Just last night. Late. If they weren't willing to

pay so dang much for a good bale of horse hay down there, I'd find somewhere other than Florida to sell it. Takes me a few days to catch up on my beauty sleep.''

''Not that you're vain or anything.'' Cleeve Harper ran a dairy on the other side of the county. He was the closest thing John had to a best friend, if men admitted to such things. They'd known each other since the first day of first grade, had both been into horses and cattle when other boys they'd grown up with had been playing with construction sets and footballs.

''You gotta admit it'll be interesting to see how all those girls turned out tonight.''

John tipped the bill of his baseball cap back, rubbed the spot in the center of his forehead where a dull ache had begun. ''There's that, I guess.''

Cleeve chuckled. ''So you think she'll—''

The cell phone squawked, then blanked out for a second.

''I didn't catch that,'' John said when it cleared up again.

''I said, do you think she'll come?''

''Who?''

''You know who.''

Just the words sent a warning signal off inside John. All his vital organs seemed to have locked up, and breathing suddenly required a conscious effort. ''Why're you askin'?''

"I actually got a chance to watch her on that news show while I was waiting on somebody yesterday morning. She's pretty damn good. And *good day,* she turned out to be a beautiful woman."

"Yeah?" John tried for indifference. The few times he had accidentally caught a glimpse of her on TV, he had seen very little in Olivia Ashford, cable news anchor, to remind him of the girl he had known. But then he'd wondered if that girl had ever existed outside his imagination, anyway.

"I wouldn't worry about it. I'm sure she's too busy with the glamorous life to come to a high-school reunion."

"No doubt." John aimed the subject in another direction altogether. "Macy comin' with you to-morrow night?"

"Hell, I don't know, John. Half the time I don't know whether she's even coming home at night."

"You in the mood for a lecture?"

"Nope."

"Well, let me know when you are." Cleeve had a knack for picking women who needed fixing, the majority of whom seemed to always end up on the other side of just-beyond-repair.

"Those calves are ready for you to pick up." Cleeve said, his turn to change the subject.

"I'll probably get over there this weekend. Maybe on Saturday."

"All right then. See ya tonight."

"Yeah, see ya." John snapped the phone shut, shoved it in his pocket and refused to stew over Cleeve's wife and the rumors that kept crossing his path when they were the last thing he wanted to hear. Besides, he couldn't get away with crediting the burning in his stomach to the woman he personally thought was making his best friend miserable. No, that went to another woman. To his left, the breeze caught the flag on top of one of the big white tents and flapped it back and forth, while his thoughts went swerving to the part of the conversation that had shaken him up inside like a runaway roller coaster.

In truth, it had never even occurred to him that Olivia Ashford might come this weekend. Had he thought it the remotest of possibilities, he would never have agreed to have the reunion here, much less be anywhere within the vicinity himself.

But there'd been no reason even to entertain the notion. She had left Summerville without so much as a backward glance just a few weeks after graduation, and in all the years since, he tried not to think about her. Ever.

There were just some things in life better left alone. For him, this was one.

"Daddy!" Flora hung halfway out the screen door at the back of the house, waving at him. "Aunt Sophia says the cookies are getting cold!"

The impatient summons from his seven-year-old

daughter reminded John that he was standing in the middle of his front yard, dwelling on a past that had nothing to do with the present—a past that no longer mattered. He waved at Flora. ''Be right there!'' he said, and headed across the yard. Olivia Ashford wasn't even real to him, anymore. She was just a memory.

Nothing more than a memory.

CHAPTER THREE

Starting Points

CLEEVE HARPER DROPPED his cell phone into the front zipper pocket of his overalls, leaving the antennae sticking out one side. The reception here on the farm was hit or miss at best, and he'd taken to driving around in the air-conditioned interior of his tractor with his phone pointed toward the heavens like the new-millennium farmer he was, as if to miss one call would send his crops into a tailspin.

Summerville's very own *GQ* farmer. That was what John called him. He'd even taken a picture of Cleeve one afternoon planting corn and sent it in to the *County Times*. Cleeve still owed him for that one, matter of fact.

He and John had always been that way with one another, ever in search of the next one-up. They were like brothers, looking out for each other as brothers would. It was this, and only this, behind John's thinly disguised disapproval of Cleeve's two-year marriage to Macy. Not a doubt in Cleeve's mind as to the truth of that, and still, it stung in the way of something a man knows to be true but just isn't ready to face up to yet.

Of course, John had his own off-limit subjects. And Olivia Ashford was one of them. What had possessed Cleeve to needle him about her this afternoon, he didn't know. Maybe it was just seeing her on TV and thinking it was a shame they had gone their separate ways all those years ago. If any two people had ever belonged together, he'd have said it was the two of them.

But then with his track record, he wasn't likely to be asked to talk to Oprah's audience on the subject of relationships.

Cleeve trudged up the brick walkway that wound through the backyard to his house, kicking red mud from his boots as he went. A short hallway led to the kitchen where Macy sat at the kitchen table, checkbook and calculator in front of her, a weekend-size suitcase on the floor beside her.

Not this again.

She looked up, the neutral expression she'd been wearing changing in an instant to one of displeasure. "Cleeve. How many times do I have to tell you to take your boots off before you come in this house? You're getting that awful red clay all over everything. And you know how impossible it is to get out."

Cleeve looked down at his boots, the sides refusing to let go of a clump or two of dirt. For the first year of their marriage, he'd done what she asked, taking the dang things on and off so many times during the course of a day that he'd practically gotten dizzy from it. Macy liked a clean house. Not exactly something he could fault her for, but what he had initially taken as a wife's admirable desire to keep an orderly home, he now realized was more about controlling his every move than anything else.

"Where you headed, Macy?"

"To visit Eileen."

"But I asked you to go to my class reunion with me."

"Cleeve." Her drawn out use of his name implied that he'd just managed to make the world's dumbest assumption. "I haven't seen my sister in weeks. And besides, those are all people you went to school with. What in the world would I have in common with them?"

"You married me?"

She sent him a look from under her lashes that underlined her previous implication. "Would you want to spend an entire weekend at one of my reunions?"

"If you wanted me to be there, yes." Cleeve folded his arms across his chest and studied her. Sometimes he wondered if he had any idea who she was. This was his third marriage, ashamed as he was of that fact, and he'd been hell-bent and determined this one was going to work. He'd met Macy at church at one of those group-counseling sessions for divorced people trying to figure out how not to get themselves in the same predicament again. They'd only dated a few months, but he'd been sure she was the one. Macy was completely different from any other woman he'd ever been involved with. Serious. Responsible. Only recently had he begun to wonder if he'd been mistaken. Pious and domineering might be better descriptions.

He sighed, pulled a glass from the cupboard by the sink and filled it with water from the tap, taking a few substantial swigs as if he could somehow douse the anger simmering inside him.

"Can't you use one of those paper cups I leave on the counter for you?" Macy asked, her voice heavy with the burden of his sin. "I just finished doing up all the dishes, and now there's another glass to wash before I go."

Cleeve swung around, his gaze clashing with the disapproving one of his wife. He was going to his high-school reunion tonight. A milestone of sorts. Fifteen years ago, he would never have believed he'd end up here. If someone had given him a crystal ball and let him take a look at what lay ahead he'd have denied the possibility of this being his life. I'd never be that stupid, he would have said.

He would have been wrong.

"Have a good weekend, Macy," he said, plop-

ping the glass on the counter, then stomping down
the hall and out the back door, glad of the trail of
red dirt he'd left behind.

RACINE DELANEY was looking for a special dress. A
wow-'em dress. A dress that said, "Bet you didn't
know I could look like this."

   She just hoped there was one in Joanne's Fine
Things—Summerville's only specialty boutique—
that she could afford.

   She pulled a sleeveless periwinkle-blue filmy
thing from the rack and held it up for a better look,
a hand at shoulder and hem. Not bad. Not stunning,
either. But then with a chest as flat as hers, and a
face that was no longer wrinkle-free, who was ever
going to call her stunning, anyway?

   It was exactly the kind of dress she'd hoped to
find, not too sexy, but alluring in a simple way.

   What the heck did she know about such things?
A girl who'd lived most of her adult life in a mobile
home with her very own conditioned response to
tremble as soon as her husband's car pulled into the
driveway. No more, though. That was over. The end.
And she was determined to find some happiness for
herself. Maybe she'd meet someone this weekend.
Someone nice. Someone interested in living life like
it was a picnic instead of a war zone.

   A diesel truck rumbled down the street outside
the shop. She glanced out the window and recog-

nized Cleeve Harper's silver Ford pickup, the twang of some top-forty country tune loud enough to damage ear drums. She wondered what he was trying to drown out.

"Hello, Racine. Could I help you with something?"

Racine looked away from the window. Joanne Norman hovered nearby. Her voice dripped honey, which seemed appropriate since her short, round frame resembled that of a bumblebee in the black-and-yellow-striped skirt and sweater she wore. Racine had never felt comfortable in this store, aware that Joanne's eyes always seemed to question whether or not she could really pay for whatever it was she'd picked out.

"I, ah, thought I might try this on."

"It's lovely," Joanne said. "Although not the most practical buy in the shop at that price."

"I'm not really looking for practical," Racine said, even as she heard the curiosity in the other woman's voice. No doubt Joanne was wondering what a woman who worked in the post office sorting mail would be doing with a dress like that.

Joanne pulled a pink cotton skirt and blouse off the rack in front of her. Sweet. Sunday-schoolish. "This is really cute."

It *was* cute. Much more like something she might have ordinarily picked out. She wavered a moment, sending a doubtful glance over the periwinkle blue.

Maybe she was being silly to think she could pull off a dress like that. But she didn't want cute today.

"I'll think about it, Joanne," she said, taking the pink outfit and draping it across the chair beside her.

"You do that. And let me know if I can help with anything else," she said, heading for the register where a short, white-haired lady was waiting to pay for a scarf.

She glanced toward the window again. Cleeve had stopped at the gas station across the street. He was talking to Leroy Jones, who'd been running the gas station as far back as her memory went. Cleeve's back was to her, and she noticed he had nice wide shoulders. He had changed little, if any, since their high-school days. On the outside, anyway. Why was it that guys like Cleeve always ended up with women like Macy?

But then if anybody understood putting up with the faults of a spouse, Racine did. There was always tomorrow, and it was sometimes easier to convince yourself it would get better by then than it was to walk away.

A long time ago, Racine had been more than a little smitten with Cleeve and had almost gotten up the nerve to flirt with him the summer before their senior year at a picnic out at Carson Lake. But she'd lost her courage, and looking back on it now, she knew he wouldn't have given her a second glance.

Guys like Cleeve had been way out of her league then. And were now.

She sent a glance back out the window where he was still talking with Leroy and then held the dress up to the mirror again. Was she really asking for anything so extraordinary? Just a good man who maybe saw something a little bit special in her? She'd once had some pretty lofty dreams. But her wants in life had gotten a lot simpler. And if she'd learned one thing in all those years since they'd left high school, it was that there was no point in wasting time wanting things you could never have.

THE SIGN WAS the same. Rolling Hills Farm. The Rileys. Since 1918. Hand-carved on dark cherry wood and mounted on one of two matching brick columns that marked the entrance to one of the prettiest pieces of land Olivia had ever seen. It hadn't changed. The name fit the farm. Two hundred acres or so of virtually flat pastures surrounded by a background of rolling hillsides that amounted to a sum total of a little over a thousand acres, if she remembered correctly.

She had arrived in Summerville late that afternoon after the four-hour drive from D.C., then checked into Lavender House, the bed-and-breakfast where she was staying for the weekend. Michael was driving down Saturday morning. She'd tried to talk him out of it since he had a couple of work commitments that prevented him from coming before then.

"You cannot go to a fifteen-year reunion without a date!" he had insisted. "Not done. Unacceptable."

She'd given in, finally. Now, she wished he'd come with her today. The message from Lori waiting at the front desk had nearly made her repack her car and head back up the interstate.

Of all places, why did the thing have to be moved to John's farm? Of all places!

She'd tried calling Lori several times, only to get her answering machine. Not surprising. As the main organizer of the reunion, she'd no doubt left hours before.

Olivia had succumbed to a long shower and set about calming the flock of internal butterflies making her nearly lightheaded. There was a single question reverberating in her head: *How could she possibly go out to Rolling Hills?*

His wife would be there. And children. What about children?

Of course, he would have children. Maybe even teenagers.

Heavens, they were old enough for that.

The possibility peeled back a few layers of indifference beneath which lay a reserve of pain left untapped for years on end. It wasn't as if she hadn't thought of it. But somehow, here, with the imminent possibility of seeing them—at his home—the prospect cut deep.

But then she'd come here looking for closure, hadn't she? Here was her chance. Had she really thought anything about it would be easy?

She was certain John hadn't given her a second's extra thought, but had gone on with his life, living it the way people do.

On that note, she had gotten dressed and left the bed-and-breakfast before she could change her mind, pointing her car down roads she remembered as if she'd driven them yesterday. Rationalizing the entire way that John probably hadn't even aged well, had gained forty pounds, or lost hair. In all reality, she wouldn't even recognize him.

Outside of storybooks, wasn't that the way real life usually worked?

Olivia parked her car near the farm's entrance sign, got out, quickly hit the remote security alarm out of habit, and set off up the asphalt road. No backing out now. She had never imagined walking up this driveway again. The years rolled back now like the curtain at a Saturday afternoon matinee, and she saw herself getting off a Greyhound bus on a cold January afternoon, her too-thin wool coat inadequate protection against the wind cutting into her skin. She'd walked the four miles from the bus station out to Rolling Hills, her heart sticking in her

throat every time she heard a car coming, terrified
one of them might be her father.

The impetus propelling her down that long road
to John's house had been some comic-Cinderella notion that he could fix what was broken inside her.
But any hope of that had collapsed beneath the reality of John's front door being answered by someone with smooth, beautiful skin, dark liquid hair.
Someone who called herself John's wife. "He and
his father have gone to a horse show this weekend
up in Culpepper," she'd said, the words clear to
Olivia's disbelieving ears. "Is there anything I can
help you with?"

"No," she had said. "No."

"Can I tell him who stopped by?"

"Just Olivia," she said. "Just tell him Olivia."

Fifteen years, and here she was again, forcing herself to put one foot in front of the other and just
walk. *Don't think. Just walk.*

Three hundred and ninety-eight steps—she
counted every one of them—and she was at the top
of the driveway. Four white tents had transformed
the front yard of the house. Cars were parked on
both sides of the road. There were people everywhere, under the tents, leaning against the board
fence, sitting beneath a couple of huge old maple
trees.

She stopped at the edge of the yard and drew in
a deep breath.

A sign-in table was positioned at the entrance. Banners in school colors of red and white hung above. Lanford County High—Class Reunion! Welcome!

And on a smaller banner below: We're Only as Old as We Think We Are!

Olivia smiled, swept back on a sudden recollection of the time John had run for class president, and she and Lori had covered the halls with posters declaring him the *only* choice. They'd spent a weekend at Lori's house coming up with all sorts of clever campaign slogans, some original, some not so. John and Cleeve had come by at regular intervals, bringing them ice-cream cones from the local Dairy Queen, and John would steal Olivia away for a few minutes, pulling her out behind the old sycamore tree in Lori's parents' backyard and hauling her into his arms for the kind of kiss that made her forget all about their campaign efforts.

"Oh, my gosh, that's Olivia Ashford!"

Two women shot across the grass like arrows from a bow, welcoming smiles on their faces.

"My goodness, I can't believe you're here!" the one in front said. "Nobody thought you would actually come."

Olivia smiled back, studying their faces for a moment before recognition hit her. "Casey. Sarah," she said. "How are you?"

Casey had ridden Olivia's school bus, Sarah had been in her homeroom.

They all hugged, then stood back to take a look at one another.

"Great. And no need to ask you that," Sarah said.

"We are so proud of you," Casey added. "Wow. You look so different in real life. Less serious, I mean. Who would ever have thought that you...I mean anyone from Summerville would end up on television every morning?"

Olivia smiled and steered the conversation away from herself. "So tell me what you're doing. Are you living in Summerville?"

"Yep," Sarah said. "Never left. I have three children, Casey has four."

"You never married, did you?" Casey asked.

"No, I never did."

"Well, with all the excitement in your life, who needs marriage and children?"

Olivia smiled again as the two women moved ahead in line. Their words settled over her with the implication that, despite all the opportunities her career had afforded her, she was the one who had missed out on something major.

"Olivia!"

The familiar voice sent relief flooding through her. She turned around to find Lori cutting her way through the crowd.

"Lori!" Olivia held out her hands to her old

friend. Lori took them, and they stepped into a warm hug that lasted for several long moments. Olivia's eyes grew moist; she had not expected the lump of emotion now wedged in her chest, preventing further words.

"Gosh, it's so good to see you," Lori said, when they'd stepped back to get a good look at one another.

Olivia swallowed. "You look wonderful. You've hardly changed at all," she said, wishing she hadn't waited so long for this particular reunion. Seeing Lori made all the years fall away. Just like that.

"Hah, compared to you, I don't think so."

"No, I mean it. You haven't changed a bit."

"A few wrinkles here and there. But we're supposed to call those character lines, aren't we?"

Olivia laughed. "I guess so."

"Obviously you got my message?"

She nodded, hoping her expression said, "No big deal."

"Were you all right with coming out here?" Lori asked with a hopeful squint.

Olivia drew in a breath. "I guess I should ask if it's all right that I'm here," she said, trying to keep the words light.

"Of course it is," Lori said, squeezing her arm while something that looked a lot like apprehension flitted across her face. "Come on, let's find a quiet spot where we can talk. We have so much to catch up on. It really is great to see you.''

They were headed to the side of the yard when a frantic voice from one of the tents called out, ''Lori, could you come up here? We've got another problem with this darn drink machine!''

Lori sighed. ''Don't they know we have fifteen years worth of stuff to catch up on?''

''You go ahead,'' Olivia said. ''We've got the whole weekend. Just look for me when you're done.''

Lori smiled and hugged her again. ''Don't go far,'' she said.

JOHN HAD NEVER been good in crowds. Especially big ones. With almost three hundred people milling about his front yard, he found himself wishing Sunday would hurry up and get here so the whole thing would be over.

The caterer had set up camp near one of the pasture fences, now putting the finishing touches on the barbecue he'd been cooking since mid-morning. If it tasted as good as it smelled, he'd be a hit. A couple of mares had been glued to that section of fence for the past few hours, patiently waiting for the next round of sugar cubes the man had been slipping them on and off all day.

Opposite the barbecue was a DJ playing current top forty, the music persistent, but still enough in the background that conversation was possible. John spotted Cleeve joking with Amy Bussey and Sharon Moore who were working the front table and pinning badges with senior pictures to jacket lapels and dresses.

Cleeve glanced up, and John waved him over. He wound his way through the crowd, a white Stetson on his head, his yellow shirt and Wranglers freshly pressed. He was tall and lean with long legs that made him a natural in the cutting-horse competitions he made time to attend in the summers with John. He had the kind of face that would never look its age. Women called him boyish. It made Cleeve madder than a hornet, but as the years ticked by, he was starting to believe John's admonishment that it wasn't such a bad tag to have hung on you.

"Don't tell me you're going to stand over here in the shadows all night," Cleeve said, giving him a shoulder joust and then an elbow jab to the ribs.

"Giving it serious consideration."

"What? You mind beating women off with a stick?"

John gave him a sideways look and rolled his eyes.

"Even as we speak, plots are being hatched in the ladies' room as to correcting your bachelor status," Cleeve said with a grin.

"Widower status."

Cleeve instantly sobered. "Ah, hell, John, that was damn callous of me. I'm sorry."

"Forget it," John said, letting out a long sigh. "Don't pay any attention to my bark. I'm not fit company for being out in public."

"Have to say, I was kind of surprised to see you down here already. Figured I'd have to come up there and reel you out of the house."

"Sophia took care of it for you."

"That's my girl," Cleeve said, his smile back.

John shook his head and gave Cleeve a once-over. "Aren't you lookin' spiffy tonight? I hardly recognized you without the cow manure on your shirt."

"Figured I might as well show some of these gals what they missed out on."

"Since you dated half the class, I guess you better get started."

To Cleeve, this was compliment, not insult. He laughed.

"So where's the one you married?" John asked.

Cleeve's smile faded. "Visiting her sister."

At the look in his friend's eyes, John was sorry he'd brought it up. "Then I guess you'll have to dance with some of these other gals, huh?"

"Guess I will," Cleeve agreed, but with less pluck than before.

"Hey, guys." Lori Peters stepped up and gave them both a hug.

John leaned back and gave her a long look. She

had on a blue cotton sundress that picked up the color of her eyes and did nice things for her fair skin. "You look great," he said.

Cleeve gave her a low wolf-whistle. "I'll second."

"You two are just used to seeing me with four kids climbing all over me," she said, glancing over her shoulder at the sign-in table where people were still filing in.

"I liked that look on you," Cleeve said.

Lori smiled, but it was a noticeably weak attempt. "John, I need to talk to you about something."

"You run the well dry? Somebody steal my best cow?"

"Not exactly," she said, her teeth catching the edge of her lower lip.

Cleeve tipped his Stetson back. "Want me to vamoose?"

"You might as well hear it, too," Lori said, throwing another uneasy glance over her shoulder. "I should have told you this earlier, this morning when I called, but I chickened out, and I know it was wrong—"

John's gaze followed hers to the edge of the yard, and the rest of whatever Lori was saying was lost to him. The plastic cup in his hand slid from his fingers and dropped to the ground, iced tea splattering his jeans and Lori's bare legs.

Cleeve put a hand on his shoulder. "What is it?

You look like you just saw a ghost.'' And then, ''Holy smoke.''

John went numb. He felt like a teenage boy again, spotting for the first time the prettiest girl he'd ever laid eyes on, hit with an immediate blood-heating attraction that fills a boy with the absolute certainty that she is the one, and imbues in him the instant inability to speak in front of her.

His first uncensored thought? Cleeve was right.

She had turned out to be one beautiful woman.

Her hair was still long, shoulder-length and blond. His fingertips instantly ached with remembrance of it.

She was leaner than she'd been then, the bone structure in her face clearly defined with angles and hollows. Her lips were the same though, a shapely, full mouth that made his own throb with sudden memory.

But one difference was apparent. She no longer looked like the small-town girl he'd dated and loved. She looked, instead, like a woman who had made it in the world—clothes, posture, the whole picture.

''What is she doing here?'' He tried to inject thunder in his voice and heard his own failure. He sounded like he'd just had the breath knocked out of him.

''That's what I was trying to tell you.'' Clearly, Lori had no idea how to handle this. She looked as if she thought he might strangle her. ''I should have told you this morning," she said, "but I was afraid you'd say no to letting us move the reunion out here if I did."

"And you would have been right!" The anger hit him full blast then. There was thunder in his voice now. And plenty of it. "Damn it all to hell, Lori. She can't stay. She cannot stay," he said, unable to bring himself to say her name because to do so would drive a knife right through the heart of the fury that was the only thing keeping his knees from buckling. "Go tell her. Now."

Lori shot him a look that somehow managed to convey both panic and absolute horror. "John! I can't possibly do that. You're blowing this out of all proportion."

"Now wait a dadblame minute," Cleeve began, reason in his voice. "She's no different from any-body else here who was in our class."

"She *is* different," John said, hearing the steel in his own words. "Either tell her, now, Lori, or the whole weekend is off."

"For Pete's sake, John," Cleeve said, "that was all a long time ago."

"Not long enough."

"You don't have to talk to her!" Lori said, hands splayed in appeal. "I'll make sure you're never within fifty yards of one another. We can't just ask her to leave."

"Nobody's askin' you to throw down the welcome mat for her,'' Cleeve tossed out, tipping back his hat, ''but you can't kick her out.''

They didn't understand. They couldn't understand. ''She isn't welcome here! And if you won't tell her, I'll tell her myself.''

CHAPTER FOUR

The Unwelcome Mat

THE LAST THING Olivia wanted was to be the center of attention. She wanted to blend in, just walk around and say hello to people she hadn't seen in nearly half a lifetime. But she had only moved a few steps past the front table since she'd arrived. There were so many people she hadn't thought about in ages, and yet remembered as if they'd seen each other only yesterday. Tommy Radcliffe, whom she'd sat beside in ninth-grade science class and shared homework notes with. Sarah Martin from eleventh-grade P.E., the only girl to consistently beat her at the six-hundred-yard dash. Noah Dumfrey who had ridden her school bus and whom she still hadn't forgiven for putting chewing gum in her hair in eighth grade. "I can't believe I actually did that to someone who's now on TV every morning!" he'd said upon seeing her, reeling her in for a hug against his now well-cushioned chest.

Most people simply looked like adult versions of

the children they had once been—some heavier, some thinner, some with gray hair, some with no hair at all. But they all looked at her differently now, with awe on their faces, as if they could no longer see the Olivia Ashford they'd known in the woman she was now.

And while it was good to see so many familiar faces, hear so many still-recognizable voices, her gaze kept skipping across the crowd. She glanced at her watch. Nine o'clock, and she still hadn't caught a glimpse of John. If she could just get that part over with, she could relax. Seeing him was inevitable, and the longer the wait drew out, the heavier her dread became.

She envisioned the two of them circling the crowd, weaving in and out until they finally ran head on into one another. Olivia could not picture him as he would look now. Couldn't imagine how time would have changed him. She found herself studying the face of every man who walked by.

How would she know him?

And then, suddenly, she didn't have to wonder anymore.

Because there he was. Cutting a path through the crowd with long strides, his mouth set in a grim, no-nonsense line.

Olivia froze, shut down inside. And then her heart took off in an out-of-control gallop that would have

made her EKG reading look like a seismograph
monitoring an L.A. earthquake.

Any semblance of poise she might have gained in
her years as a professional broadcaster completely
deserted her. She stood in front of him as vulnerable
as if she were seventeen again and head over heels
in love. She couldn't smile. Couldn't speak.
Couldn't move.

He didn't look old.

He hadn't gained forty pounds.

He had all his hair.

And she would have recognized him in a crowd
of a thousand on the other side of the world.

To say he looked good would have been an understatement.

Living in Washington, D. C., Olivia had gotten
used to men in suits. The professional man's uni-
form: polished loafers, socks with crests on them,
starched white shirts, hundred-dollar ties. Washington was full of men like that. That was the kind of
man today's women were supposed to find irresistible.

She never had.

And now she realized why.

Because she would forever be comparing them to
John. But John Riley as a boy was quite different
from John Riley as a man.

There was no questioning which one he was now.

His shoulders had gotten broader. He was more

muscular, solid, strong. The changes were unsettling, maybe because *that* John, she knew. This one, she did not. And the reality of him, standing here in front of her, felt like a kaleidoscope of then and now.

"Olivia."

At the sound of his voice, she jumped. Olivia. Not Liv as she had once been to him. The greeting was arctic-cold, his whole demeanor one of stiff politeness as if he'd just bumped into someone he had vaguely known in first grade, but wasn't quite sure he remembered.

"Hello, John." She folded her arms across her chest to hide her shaking hands. The urge to flee was nearly irresistible. All of a sudden, she felt like a country girl who'd never been farther than twenty-five miles outside Summerville, who had grown up in a four-room house and gotten her new clothes from the church's Helping Hand closet.

"Mind if I ask what you're doing here?" The question was clipped, his anger barely concealed.

Olivia's stomach did a roller-coaster plummet at the recognition of it. She locked her knees and forced herself to return his scrutiny.

People were staring. She felt their curious gazes. Heard the whispers. She willed her voice toward something close to indifference when she said, "The same thing as everyone else in our class."

"Everyone else is welcome here."

The words snagged her like barbed wire, cutting through the skin and refusing to let go, their harshness in opposition to the boy she had once known, a boy whose eyes had looked at her as if she were every good thing he'd ever imagined. A flash of memory hit her. The two of them up on Lookout Mountain, lying on their backs in the bed of his old pickup, a quilt beneath them, staring up at the stars and holding hands. Her head was on his shoulder. Amazing that with all the time that had passed since then, she still remembered the depth of the security she'd felt there. *I want us to have four children, Liv. At least four. That way they'll never grow up lonely. Days like Christmas will be loud and out of control. I like out of control.*

Had he really said words like that to her, this man with undiluted disapproval in his eyes?

It didn't seem possible.

She hated herself, suddenly, for the inability to forget, as he so obviously had. There was no doubt that he had put away all the good memories and had no interest in revisiting any of them.

He stood, arms folded across his chest, waiting for her to respond.

Her lips moved although she had no idea what words they were going to form. "I have every right to be here at this reunion, John," she said, keeping her voice low. "But this is your home, and I'm sorry if I've made you uncomfortable by coming here."

"I'm not uncomfortable," he said, the denial instant. "Surprised. I never imagined you'd have that much nerve."

His directness toppled her poise. "I didn't know the reunion had been moved until this afternoon—"

"But you still came."

Again, the words fired at her like missiles with computer-targeted aim. She felt under assault. Countless times, she had imagined what it would be like to see him again. What she would say. How she would feel. None of her scenarios had ever depicted John angry. Indifferent, yes. But not angry. He had married someone else within six months of her leaving here. Why would a man who had forgotten her that quickly have an ounce of anger inside him?

"Just as long as you know this," he said, before she could manage to respond. "Your being here makes no difference whatsoever to me. Let's just make sure we let this be both hello and goodbye, okay?"

And with that, he left her standing there, cutting his way back through the hovering crowd of slack-jawed classmates who had sidled in close enough not to miss a word.

JOHN GRABBED a glass from the cabinet above the kitchen sink, flipped the tap on, then downed several swallows of cold water. He set the glass down on the counter, braced his hands on the sink's edge, head down, yanking air into his lungs. Over the years, he'd done some serious speculating about what it would be like to see Liv again. None of his scenarios had ever even hinted at the reality of it, at the fact that standing there in front of her, close enough to touch her, close enough to see confusion in her eyes, was like having someone drive a semi straight through the wall of his chest.

He'd expected to be protected by his own indifference, had wrapped himself up in it. Liv hadn't spoken five words before the edges unraveled, leaving him completely vulnerable, and it would be a long time before he thawed out again.

"What on earth are you doing in here when there's a party going on outside?"

John looked over his shoulder. Sophia stood in the kitchen doorway, the frown on her face the same one she'd been giving him for suspicious behavior since he was ten years old. When John's mother had died, Sophia, his father's sister, had come to live with them. Since Laura's death, she had also become so important to Flora that John couldn't imagine either of them getting along without her. "Just biding time, Sophia," he said.

"You planning to stand there all weekend?"

"Might."

"Then you won't be setting your sights on Most Sociable, I take it."

"I had about all I could handle," he said, ignoring her smile.

"So what are you going to do about the rest of the weekend?"

"The view from here looks pretty good."

Sophia chuckled and pulled a clean apron from one of the cabinet drawers, gave it a shake and tied it around her waist. "So she did come then?" She reached for a dishtowel and began drying the few bowls that had been left to drain in the sink. The question came totally without fanfare, as if she had just asked him whether he'd remembered to pick up some milk when he'd run into town earlier that afternoon.

"Who?" John asked, neutralizing his expression.

"You know good and well who."

As much as John loved Sophia, he did not, at that moment, appreciate her uncanny ability to cut to the heart of things. He avoided her gaze, glaring, instead, at the row of pink sponge curlers on the left side of her head. "I told her she wasn't welcome here."

Sophia uttered something that sounded like a snort and flapped her dishtowel. "John Crawford Riley! Where are your manners? You were not raised like that."

"She showed up at this house uninvited," he dug in.

"She *was* invited," Sophia reasoned. "She's a

member of this class just like you were. And if you were indifferent to the girl, you wouldn't care whether she was here or not.'' For emphasis, she plunked a just-dried cup in the cabinet above her head.

John gave her sponge curlers another glare. It was hard to argue with Sophia on this subject. She was, after all, the one who had found him in his room, spilling tears all over Liv's picture after she'd left Summerville. He wasn't going to fool her. Nor was he going to give her the satisfaction of saying she was right.

"But I suppose you could make her believe you care if you had a mind to." She put down the towel and turned to look at him.

John shot her another narrow-eyed glare. "What do you mean?"

"I mean that if you hide out in the house all weekend, it's going to be pretty clear to everybody that you never got over her."

Something exploded inside him. "If you think I've given her a second thought in all these years—"

"You were a good husband, John," Sophia interrupted in a quiet, firm voice. "I'm not accusing you of anything. But I know what that girl once meant to you. And now here she is on this farm again. Don't tell me you haven't thought about her. You're human, aren't you?"

"She wasn't who I thought she was."

Sophia untied her apron and put it away. She reached for a glass from the cabinet by the sink, filled it with water from the faucet. "This weekend could be a bridge in your life, John Riley, maybe even make you want to live again. You just think about that." She left the kitchen.

John glared at her retreating shoulders. He had every right to mind the fact that Liv Ashford would just show up here after the way she had left and never called, never written. It had been years before he'd even heard where she was living. Someone had seen her on a local news channel in Johnson City, and the rumor had spread through Summerville until it had reached him one afternoon when he'd been in the hardware store with Laura buying a new light fixture for the back porch. Lenny Nelson had no way of knowing what the information would do to John, no way of guessing he might as well have stuck a knife inside him. John had paid for the light fixture, smiled and said, "Oh, really, well, that's great!" while Laura listened with mild interest, and his heart was being torn right out of his chest.

It wasn't the first or the last time he had questioned whether emotional infidelity was any less wrong than physical.

How many times had Laura said "I love you," and he'd tried to say it back with the same conviction? How did he explain the regret he felt now for not having given her the same kind of love she had given him, uncluttered by something that could have been, that never was? He still lay awake at night, cursing himself for not making their marriage what it should have been.

And yet, Laura had never made it an issue between them. She had been aware that there had been someone else not long before she'd come into his life, although she hadn't found out about Liv until after they were married. She'd run across a shoebox of old letters one day while cleaning out the attic. They were letters from Liv, which he'd had no business keeping but hadn't been able to throw away. Liv had written him notes in school, putting them in places where he would find them throughout the day, in his science book, his locker, the front seat of his truck. Some of them had been no more than a line long: *Hey, just thinking about you!* And some of them longer: *So that's what it's like to be kissed by someone you want to spend the rest of your life with. Highly recommended.*

He could still remember so many of them line by line.

He remembered the look in Laura's eyes when she'd admitted to reading them—understanding tinted with sadness and resignation, and awareness that what had come before her would always be between them.

It had been almost two years since Laura had

died. If he could give her nothing else, he would make sure that everyone at this damned reunion knew he had loved her. That she had been his wife. The mother of his daughter. The one who counted.

He owed her that much.

And Sophia was right about one thing. He wasn't going to prove any of that by standing up here acting like he cared whether Liv Ashford had waltzed herself back into town or not.

So he yanked open the back door with enough force to make the old hinges groan and headed outside.

OLIVIA MADE her way to the back of the house, keeping her head down to avoid meeting anyone's eyes, grateful for the darkness that concealed her from view. A few minutes to get herself together, and she would be fine. Just fine.

What in the world had she been thinking?

Coming back here had been nothing but a mistake. How could she have believed anything else?

Once, she'd had a panic attack on a crowded elevator in an Atlanta bank. She'd been standing in the back, and it had hit her before she ever saw it coming, tightening her chest, refusing to let air in her lungs.

That's how she felt now. As if breathing had become something she had to think out second by second.

Tall, old oak trees threw evening shadows across the backyard. Wrought-iron chairs were arranged in a circle on the brick patio. Olivia pulled one away from the halo of light dancing out from the lanterns hanging by the French doors. She sat down and dropped her head onto her hands.

How could something still hurt this much after so long? She had not seen John Riley in fifteen years, and in all that time her heart had not gained an ounce of immunity to him.

"Whatcha doin'?"

Olivia shot up from the chair and whirled around. A small face stared down at her from the second story of the house, the curious eyes disturbingly familiar.

"Oh. I was just..."

"You're crying."

"No. I...well, not really."

The little girl disappeared from the window, popped back seconds later and said, "Here."

Two tissues floated down. Olivia caught them. "Thank you."

"They're the soft kind. Are you sad?"

This was John's child. If Olivia had not been able to tell from the eyes alone, her shoot-from-the-hip manner would have been a dead giveaway. "A little, I guess."

"It's okay to be sad. That's what Aunt Sophia

says. And she says sadness can't get better until you 'knowledge it's there.''

A name from the past. How many afternoons had she come with John to this house after school where they would do their homework at the kitchen table while Sophia fixed dinner? Olivia had helped her peel potatoes or shred lettuce for a salad. Sophia had taught her how to make homemade biscuits. They were John's favorite, and he'd made her promise she would make them every morning for breakfast after they got married. After leaving Summerville, Olivia had never made biscuits again. ''Sophia is a wise woman,'' she said.

''She's real smart.'' The little girl nodded, rubbing an eye with the back of a small hand. ''My mommy died. I've been sad a lot. I think my daddy has been, too. Only he won't admit it.''

Olivia took a step back. Shock ricocheted through her like a stone skimming the surface of a pond. Laura Riley had died. That pretty girl who had answered the door on a winter afternoon so long ago was dead. John's wife.

How many times had she imagined the kind of life John would have had with Laura? Imagined her being the kind of woman who sent him off each morning with a hot breakfast and greeted him at the door each night with the smell of bread wafting from the oven.

The wondering seemed trivial now, intrusive even.

She took a deep breath and finally managed, "I'm so sorry."

"She was a good mommy."

"I'm sure she was," Olivia said, her throat so tight she was surprised the words had actually made their way out.

"Daddy says she's in heaven, and that it's a good place. He says she gets to have her real hair there, and she won't even have to chew sugarless gum. She can have real bubble gum."

Olivia's heart contracted. "That's nice, isn't it?"

She nodded. "But I wish she didn't have to go. I miss her. Daddy says God sometimes takes the good people and leaves the rest here to give them a chance to figure out how to be that way. I'm not good sometimes 'cause I don't want to leave Daddy. He needs me. Every once in a while I won't eat all my dinner or forget to make up my bed."

"I bet God understands." Olivia swallowed hard at the little girl's matter-of-fact assessment. "What's your name?"

"Flora. What's yours?"

"Olivia."

"That's pretty."

"Thank you. So's Flora."

A black nose appeared in the window and nudged Flora's arm aside. "We woke up Charlie."

"I see we did." Olivia peered up at the golden retriever now framed in the window beside Flora.

"It's Charlie, short for Charlene. A lot of people think it's weird for her to have a boy's name since she's a girl."

"I think Charlie's a good name."

"She sleeps with me in case I have a bad dream at night."

"It looks like you're in awfully good hands."

The dog licked Flora's face, obviously aware she was being discussed. Flora giggled again. "Yuk, Charlie. We better get back to bed before Daddy sees us."

"Okay. It was nice to meet you, Flora."

"'Night."

"Good night." The window slid closed. Both little girl and dog disappeared.

A second later, the window popped back up, and the tow-headed child stuck her head out again. "Are you still sad?"

Olivia shook her head and tried to smile. "I'm better now."

Flora looked pleased. "Good. Okay. 'Night."

The window zipped back down, and she was gone, leaving Olivia's heart bruised with knowledge and a sorrow she would never have expected to feel.

CLEEVE FILED IN at the tail end of the not-insignificant line waiting at the bar. He checked his watch and angled a look across the crowd. Still no sight of John. If he didn't turn up within the next five minutes, Cleeve was going looking for him. Matter of fact, maybe he'd get the bartender to pour him a couple shots of bourbon to take along in case he found him. Granted, it was a quick fix. But John probably needed one right about now.

"Guess they gave everybody something to talk about tonight, anyway."

Cleeve turned around. Racine Delaney stood behind him, a hesitant smile on her face. "Hey, Racine."

"Hi, Cleeve."

"Guess you saw the John and Olivia thing."

"Kind of hard to miss it."

Cleeve sighed. "Yeah, he's never been real reasonable where that gal was concerned. I think he was a little caught off guard."

"I was kind of surprised to see her here."

Cleeve nodded, surprised himself to find Racine having a conversation with him. The only time he ever saw her anymore was in the post office, and for some reason, he'd never thought she liked him much. She somehow managed to dole out his book of stamps each time without quite meeting eyes with him. "So...you havin' a good time?" he asked, feeling awkward and not at all sure why.

"Uh-huh," she said, glancing around as if she were hoping somebody else would appear and save her. She lowered her gaze and smoothed a hand across her dress.

Which he noticed then for the first time. It was pretty, some odd blue that women probably had a name for. In fact, Racine looked pretty. She was an attractive woman, completely different from the girl with the thick glasses he remembered from high school. He could see she'd taken extra pains tonight. Her hair, which she normally wore pulled back in a tight ponytail, hung straight and shiny, just grazing her shoulders. "You look real nice, Racine," he said and meant it.

Her eyes lit up. And then as if catching herself, she cleared her throat and said, "Where's Macy?"

"She made other plans for the weekend."

"That's a shame," she said.

They were the kind of words that would have sounded placating from most people. But somehow, when Racine said them, it sounded like she meant them. Cleeve rolled that around for a few moments, and then, "Heard about you and Jimmy."

"About time I wised up, huh?"

"You all right?"

"Better than I've been in years."

"Jimmy had no idea what he had."

"Thank you."

"Truth doesn't need any thanks," he said. Cleeve had heard the rumors for a long time, seen Racine's attempts to cover up suspicious-looking marks on her face. And one time when he'd picked up his truck after having some work done on it, he had tried to talk to Jimmy, suggested that maybe he ought to go see somebody. Jimmy hadn't been too thrilled with the suggestion. Cleeve didn't give a hoot about that, but he'd always worried that Jimmy might have taken it out on Racine when he got home that night. It was beyond him how a man could hit a woman at all, much less one he claimed to love.

"You know, I'm not really thirsty after all," she said, backing up. "I see someone over there I wanted to say hello to. See ya, Cleeve."

"Are you sure I can't get you—" He raised a hand to stop her, but she was already gone. And he stood there wondering what he'd said to make her leave so fast.

RACINE MADE a beeline for the other side of the yard, her high heels refusing to cooperate with the speed she was asking of them. Her cheeks felt as if they'd spent a couple hours under a sun lamp. What in the world had possessed her to strike up a conversation with Cleeve Harper? She'd spotted him standing there in that line alone, and it was as if someone had thrown a cable around her neck and just steered her right over.

Oh, no, you're not getting off that easy, Racine. You wanted to talk to him! That's why you went over there.

Strangely enough, the self-chastisement had her mother's voice. Oh, boy, would she love that. Her divorced daughter flirting with a married man.

Well, it hadn't exactly been flirting. She'd just been making conversation.

So, why did you light up like the Fourth of July when he complimented your dress?

Go away, Mom.

Racine did not need her mother telling her that Cleeve Harper was nothing more than a dead-end street. She was fully aware of that fact, and she'd already taken the only dead-end street she intended to take in this lifetime.

Over by a stretch of board fence, Jerry Dunmore stood by himself nursing a can of Sprite. Voted Most Shy, it looked as if he hadn't yet managed to overcome the label. Racine put Cleeve from her mind and headed over.

CHAPTER FIVE

So That's How It Was

OLIVIA HAD JUST ventured back into the crowd of classmates in the front yard when Cleeve Harper came striding toward her, a big smile on his very unchanged face. Still numb from her encounter with John's little girl, Olivia welcomed Cleeve's all-encompassing bear hug. Her feet dangled above the ground when he said, "Still pretty as a picture."

He plunked her down, and she looked up at him with a smile. "And what's your secret against aging?"

Cleeve let out a pleased-sounding scoff. "Shoot. Wish I had one."

"You look great, Cleeve."

"Well, you're the one who's gone and made us all so dang proud."

"Thank you. That's awfully nice."

"You're good at it. Me? If I got in front of a camera with millions of people watching, I'd freeze up faster than an ice cube at the North Pole."

Olivia laughed. That had always been one of Cleeve's talents. Making people laugh. He'd had a definite way with the girls, too, which was a little surprising considering he'd grown up on a dairy farm with very strict parents and had never even been into the town of Summerville until he was eleven years old. He and John had been friends from the first day they'd met, in much the same way she and Lori had been. It might have been awkward between the two of them now, but Cleeve had never been the type to judge, and she was deeply appreciative of his acceptance of her here in light of John's obvious disapproval.

Lori jogged up just then, a few pieces of her neatly upswept hair having escaped its bobby pins. "Cleeve, have you been hogging her?"

"I just saw her," he said, indignant.

Lori gave him a playful thwap on the arm. "Likely story!" she said. And then to Olivia, "I got tied up with five different emergencies, but I've been looking all over for you. We've barely talked."

"I went for a walk," Olivia said.

Lori put a hand on her arm. "You and John all right about all this?"

"Everything's fine," Olivia said, reaching for her most convincing smile.

"Sorry he was a little less than gracious," Cleeve said. "I'm planning to turn him over my knee if I ever find him."

"That I'd like to see," Lori said. "I've just got one more thing to do, Olivia, and my duties are over for the night. This won't take but a few minutes. I promise." And then before Olivia could say anything else, Lori was headed up front to the edge of one of the big tents where a microphone and podium had been set up. She stepped behind it, picked up a piece of paper and tapped the mike.

"Attention everybody!"

The buzz of the crowd softened to a murmur.

"Senior superlatives!" Lori said, waving the paper in her hand. "Best Smile! Most Likely to Succeed! You remember! Let's see if the awards still fit!"

A collective groan went through the crowd while Olivia's stomach dropped like an elevator whose cable had just been cut. "Oh, no," she said.

"This should be good." Cleeve wiggled his eyebrows at her.

"Come on, don't tell me you haven't all been waiting for this!" Lori cajoled.

"She's enjoying this a little too much, I think."

Olivia looked over her shoulder. An attractive blond man with lively blue eyes and small wire-framed glasses smiled at her. "I'm Sam Peters. Lori's husband. And you're Olivia."

"Sam. It's so nice to meet you," she said, turning to clasp his outstretched hand between her own two.

"Hey, Cleeve," Sam said.

"Hey, Sam. You're right. Your wife is enjoying this. She's got that gleam in her eye."

"Know that means trouble."

Both men laughed.

"I've heard an awful lot about you over the years, Olivia," Sam said, his voice appealingly deep and sincere. "It's good to finally meet you."

"You, too, Sam. Really. You're exactly what I would have imagined for Lori." And he was. A little bookish. Athletic with a winner of a smile.

He laughed. "I hope that's good."

"It is," she said.

"All right, everyone, let's get started." Lori's directive drew their attention back to the front of the crowd. En masse, the group moved in closer to the podium. Olivia wished for some discreet way of leaving, but with Cleeve and Sam on either side of her, it wasn't possible. She did a quick mental scramble for that flag of courage she'd been waving all the way from D.C.

"First off, Best Smile," Lori announced. "Tammy Young and Harry Sigmon!"

The crowd clapped and cheered while Tammy and Harry threaded their way through to the front where Lori pinned them with badges declaring their superlative. "I think they still qualify," Lori said, and indeed, the two classmates wore the kind of friendly smiles that can somehow get a person's day off to the right start.

Tammy and Harry stepped back and started a row behind Lori who again dipped her head to the microphone. "Best Sense of Humor. Sally Acres and Kip Fincastle."

Sally and Kip were standing close to Olivia. She smiled despite the buffalo-size butterflies that had taken up residence inside her. Kip carried a chair up front with him. After receiving his badge and bowing to the crowd, he held it out for Sally who sat down with an oh-thank-you look on her face. The chair made a less than polite noise. Sally shot up, reached beneath the seat and yanked out the whoopee cushion Kip had planted there.

The group erupted in laughter while Sally pretended to look shocked, but it was obvious she'd been in on the gag all along.

Olivia didn't dare look around for fear she'd meet eyes with John who was no doubt dreading what lay ahead as much as she was.

Lori announced the next two: Most Likely to Succeed, Least Likely to Change. Loud cheers and wolf whistles as these four made their way to the front.

"Most Popular," Lori said. "Cleeve Harper and Aggie Lester."

Cleeve took mock bows all the way up, offering the crowd his best Miss America wave. Still blond and pretty, Aggie was positively tame beside him. Just before they got to the stage, Cleeve swooped her off her feet and carried her the rest of the way. A wave of laughter rolled through the crowd.

Lori shook her head and said, "You should have been Least Changed, Cleeve."

"Never did like to disappoint my fans."

More laughter.

Smiling, Lori announced, "Next up, Best-looking." Whistles went up from the crowd. "That would be Olivia Ashford and John Riley."

Olivia wished she could disappear.

"Come on, now," Cleeve waved at her from up front, and then added, "Where is that boy? Get on up here, John!"

The crowd started clapping. "Whoo, John!"

Among the clapping and hoots, Olivia somehow managed to put one foot in front of the other.

Without looking, she knew John was behind her, felt his gaze on her back and the reluctance rolling off him like steam off July asphalt after a sudden thunderstorm. They both stopped just short of the microphone and waited while Lori pinned them with their badges. John had to bend forward so Lori could reach him. His shoulder brushed Olivia's, and they both jumped as if they'd been touched with a hot poker. And as they turned to take position with the other classmates on stage, their eyes met and betrayed them, failing to conceal their remembrance of the first time they'd been awarded the title. It wasn't something either one of them had taken seriously, but after the assembly was over, John had pulled her behind a set of bleachers and kissed her, teasing, "I voted for you. Who'd you vote for?"

"Pete Simmons," she'd said with mock seriousness. Pete had been their star quarterback and changed girlfriends as often as most guys changed shirts.

John had picked her up and whirled her around.

"Okay, okay," she'd said, laughing. "I didn't."

He'd put her down and kissed her again, and they'd both gotten tardy slips for being late to their next class.

"They still have it?" Lori asked the crowd, bringing Olivia back to the moment.

More hoots went up. From the women: "All right, John!" And the men: "Ooh, baby, Olivia!"

The next twenty minutes on that stage felt more like four hours, and were as awkward and uncomfortable as anything Olivia ever remembered enduring. She and John were the only two standing far enough apart not to look like a matched set, looking instead exactly what they were: two people who had been forced into a situation neither wanted to be in.

With a smile frozen on her face, Olivia ridiculed herself for ever thinking she could come back to this place and not be affected by the man next to her. It was one thing to live hundreds of miles away, far from visual proof of all that had been lost, of everything that might have been. Physical distance was a sort of anesthesia. Here, next to this man with whom she had once had every intention of sharing her life, she felt raw and exposed, every nerve ending screaming for numbness. There was none here. On some level, she had known this, had not come back before now because of it.

To be here in this place where their lives had once been entwined was to feel.

Her choices were clear: turn around and head back to shore. Or keep swimming and aim for the other side.

JOHN DIDN'T WASTE any time getting off that stage. What was it about reunions that made people come up with all sorts of masochistic ways to look back at the past?

Standing up there beside Liv had been like being subjected to one of those water-dripping tortures designed to drive a man crazy a moment at a time.

Halfway across the yard, Cleeve jogged up from behind and caught him by the arm. "Where you runnin' off to now?"

"Done for the night," John said.

"You know, this doesn't have to be such a bad thing," Cleeve said, giving him a squinty frown of disapproval. "Might even do you some good."

"How's that?"

"This is just Dr. Harper talkin' here, but I don't think you ever got over her."

"I got over her a long time ago, doc," John said, keeping the words light. "I don't need any counselin' sessions this weekend, but I do have a bottle of bourbon stored away that's been looking for an excuse to be opened."

Cleeve hesitated a moment, as if he wanted to continue the lecture, but decided to shelve it for now. "By all means," he said, "let's go give her one."

RUBY'S HADN'T CHANGED in fifteen years.

The reunion had begun to break up around eleven. When Lori suggested meeting at the café in the center of town for pie and coffee, Olivia had been glad of the opportunity for the two of them to have some time to talk.

Judging from the number of cars parked outside at this late hour, Ruby's was still the place to go for a good, reliable meal and familiar faces.

From the front entrance, Olivia took a long look, nostalgia hitting her in one of those aching waves of longing for a past that can only exist in memory.

The green vinyl booths were the same. The white tile floors cleaner than clean. Behind the front counter was the same soda fountain that had been there when she had been a little girl and a Cherry Coke had been a rare treat. The sameness of the place made her memories all the more real: she and Lori coming here after school for a milkshake and fries; she and John stopping in after a movie and sharing a banana split in the booth by the window which they'd come to think of as theirs.

She took a seat in a corner of the diner as far from that particular booth as she could get. The place was over half full. Olivia felt the not-so-subtle stares from the tables around her. She had long ago gotten used to the scrutiny that came from being recognized, but for the first time in a long while, she wished for anonymity, to sit here with her old friend and just fit in.

"Hi." Lori tossed out the greeting a few yards from the table, hung her purse on the back of the chair and sank onto the seat. "Tell me you're not mad at me for not warning you about the superlative thing."

Olivia shook her head. "Guess you knew better."

"Selfish, maybe, but I didn't want you to leave."

"And I probably would have."

Their waitress appeared, her smile quick and sincere considering the hour. "What can I get you?" she asked.

"Coffee for me," Lori said. "And what the heck? I'll have a slice of your coconut-cream pie."

"Make that two," Olivia added.

The waitress scribbled something on her pad, then glanced up. "You want cream and sugar with—"

She broke off there, recognition flooding her face. "Why you're that—You're—" She snapped her fingers. "Olivia Ashford! Well, I'll be. Marcille!" she yelled over her shoulder at the waitress taking an order from the next table over. "We've got a real celebrity in tonight!"

Marcille glanced up from her order pad, squinted at Olivia, then Lori, then returned to Olivia again. "Sure enough!"

She hustled across the room, waving her pad and saying, "Oh, could I get an autograph for my mother? She *loves* your show."

Olivia smiled, and ended up writing one out for both women, a little uncomfortable with the request simply because she wanted to be nothing other than Lori's old friend without the differences in their lives getting in the way.

Once the two enthusiastic waitresses had headed off toward the kitchen, Lori said, "I'm sorry about the scene with John."

"I should have expected it," Olivia said. She hesitated and then, "I didn't know about his wife."

Lori fiddled with the handle on her coffee cup. "I thought about telling you when I called a couple weeks ago, but I didn't know how to bring it up. Laura didn't deserve what happened to her. She was a really wonderful person."

"I'm sure she was judging by her daughter."

"You met Flora then?"

Olivia recalled the sweet face peering down at her from the bedroom window. "She's adorable."

"John is crazy about her. She's what kept him going. There's no question about that."

"Is he okay?" Olivia heard the concern in her own voice, but refused to take the time to analyze it or to try and cover it up.

"Some days, I think. It's been almost two years. It's been difficult. John hasn't changed much really. Still thinks he can handle everything himself. To be honest with you, when I asked him if we could move the reunion out to his place, I never expected him to say yes. He's pretty much isolated himself since Laura died. Doesn't go out or anything."

Olivia wanted to tell Lori she had met his wife all those years ago when she had come back, never imagining that John would have found someone else so soon. But it seemed somehow inappropriate now, an invasion of another woman's still very real presence.

"Can I ask you something, Olivia?" Lori's expression had changed. Solemn, now.

"Of course."

Lori looked down at her lap, then met Olivia's gaze, a wounded, hurt look in her eyes. "Why'd you leave without letting anybody know?"

Olivia put down her cup, studied the tabletop for a few seconds and searched for words. Of course, she had known the question was coming. What a relief it would have been to share what had happened all those years ago with Lori. What a relief it would be not to carry the weight of knowledge alone. And yet, fear kept her silent. Fear of judgment. Fear of confirmation. For and of her own responsibility in what had happened. If she had only told someone, a teacher, another parent, Lori, John…if she had only let someone know before that last awful night…then maybe things would have turned out so differently. Maybe she wouldn't have ended up in the emergency room by herself, too ashamed to call John and ask him to come. But she'd kept the secret of her home life to herself for so long that it had become second nature to her. It wouldn't be long before she would be leaving, she'd told herself, going away to college, making a life with John, a very different life where home would be a safe place, a good place. But in one night, everything had changed. Life had gone veering off on a track she had never anticipated, and sharing the burden with Lori now wouldn't change any of it.

She reached across the table and took Lori's hands between her own. "We were best friends from the day we met, right?"

"Yes," Lori said, her tone soft, concerned.

"Will you trust me then just to say that I never wanted to leave? That it was something I had to do."

Lori squeezed her hands back. "I believe you, and I don't need to know why. I'm just glad you're here.

And I hope this weekend is just a beginning, that it won't be the last time we see each other.''

Olivia's heart was full with love and affection for this woman who had once been such an important part of her life. She was sorry, truly sorry, that they had missed so many years. She didn't intend to let the future repeat the pattern. "It won't," she said. "It won't."

THEY TALKED for two hours.

About everything. Lori's children, each sounding special and unique. About her career. She'd held an important position with a pharmaceutical company until deciding to stay home with her children, at least while they were young. And how truly happy she was in her marriage. Olivia admired her more than she could say. Lori's life sounded full and fulfilling.

And maybe there was just a little envy there as well.

They talked about Olivia's life, too. The fact that she'd taken up running several years ago and had actually done a couple of marathons. About her career, how she'd moved from city to city, climbing the ladder. With the generosity that was her nature, Lori was proud of her, genuinely thrilled at her success. And they relived some old memories that made them both laugh until their sides hurt. Like the day Lori had gotten her driver's license, and they'd been awarded her mother's old green Falcon for a night on the town. Despite the rust holding the car together, they had been thrilled, sixteen and completely amazed that they were finally old enough to do such a thing. Out on the town by themselves! They'd tooled down Main Street, the radio blasting Lori's sister's Earth, Wind & Fire tape, the windows rolled down, the car backfiring every half mile or so. Their bubble had burst when they'd looked around to find a state trooper's car zooming up behind them, lights flashing.

"You remember how terrified we were?" Lori laughed and dropped her voice an octave or two. "Miss Morgan, I'm not sure which driver's education class you attended, but the idea is to stop back there on that white line. It makes it kind of hard to see when the light turns green if you're right up under it like that."

Olivia laughed now until she could hardly catch her breath.

"I want you to know that unto this day I am a model citizen when it comes to stopping on the white line," Lori said.

Olivia picked up her napkin and wiped her eyes, sobering. "Could that really have been that many years ago?"

Lori shook her head. "Life doesn't exactly sit around waiting on any of us, does it?"

"No, I'm afraid it doesn't."

They smiled at one another, and it was strange, but of all the friends and acquaintances Olivia had acquired in the life she'd made since leaving here, none of them had ever been like Lori. They'd always been this comfortable with each other. The kind of comfortable where you borrowed each other's clothes, used each other's lipstick, wore each other's shoes. Real friends with real roots. And, oh, she had missed this kind of connection.

"You're really happy with your life, aren't you, Lori?"

"I am. You know, it's funny how when we're younger, we list off all the things we want when we're adults and can do what we please. A big house, a fancy car, great clothes, an impressive job. But what gets me up every morning, what makes me feel good about myself when I go to bed at night is my husband and children. It all comes back to that."

Olivia planted her gaze on her coffee cup. The words sent a little arrow through her heart, and with it came the sudden realization of the hollowness in her own life, the distinct feeling that something was missing. She blinked and looked back up.

"Okay, everybody, five minutes to closing." Marcille made the announcement from the cash register.

Lori glanced at her watch. "Gosh, it *is* late. Can you come over to the house for lunch tomorrow?"

"I'd love to."

Lori gave her some quick directions, then picked up her purse from the floor. "I feel like I've been given a gift I thought I'd lost a long time ago. I don't want to lose it again."

"Neither do I."

"Good." She reached across the table to squeeze Olivia's hand. "Then we won't. We just won't."

To Olivia, it seemed impossible that two people could put a lost friendship back on track in so short a time when it had been left to wither for fifteen years. But that was exactly what they had done. Lori didn't need to know why. She had merely welcomed her back. Accepted her. And maybe, after all, that was the real definition of friendship.

CHAPTER SIX

Bedtime Stories

SOPHIA HAD a long-standing eight o'clock appointment every Friday morning at the So-Chic Beauty Salon in town for a wash and set.

Friday was therefore John's day to make breakfast for Flora, the menu usually consisting of either oatmeal and toast or frozen waffles with maple syrup. They were the only two breakfast foods he knew how to make. It was a good thing they both happened to be his daughter's favorites. He'd never been sure if that was actually true, or simply another of her attempts to make him feel as if he was acing this single-parent thing.

Unfortunately for him, the smell of the waffles did not appeal this morning. Between the two of them, he and Cleeve had made a good-size dent in that bottle of bourbon, the aftermath leaving John with a colossal headache that was now beating at his temples with all the subtlety of a sledgehammer.

Flora was in her chair at the center of the table.

Her brown hair hung in a braid down her back. Since it was Friday, she'd picked out her favorite outfit—faded overalls with a pink T-shirt. Laura had been against such clothes for school. She'd thought them too tomboyish, but like so many things these days, John didn't have the heart to deny his daughter this simple pleasure. And yet the needle of guilt was there, too, making him wonder if he should change something Laura had felt strongly about.

"Look, Daddy." Flora pointed her fork at the newspaper on the table in front of her. Syrup dripped off the tip and landed on the elephant pictured beneath the headline.

"Watch out, honey. You're making a mess."

Flora dabbed at the syrup with her napkin. "Sorry, Daddy," she said, looking down at her lap, her bottom lip teetering.

Regret hit John in the chest. His patience was way too thin this morning, his own rattled mind no excuse. "No, I'm sorry, sweet pea. I'm a little grumpy today."

"It's okay, Daddy," she said. "Did you stay up late last night?"

"A little bit."

"You always say I'm grumpy if I don't go to bed at my regular time."

"You're right. I do," he said.

He got up from the table, dumped his half-eaten waffles in the trash and stuck his plate in the sink.

"There was a lady outside my window last night."

"Really?" Flora had enough imagination for ten children her age, and it wasn't unusual for her to make up stories for him. He liked to hear them. In fact, most nights she told him bedtime stories before she went to sleep. She was much better at it than he was.

"Uh-huh. She was crying, so I gave her some tissues."

John dropped the dishcloth in the sink and swung around to look at his daughter. This didn't sound like a fairy tale. "What lady?"

"Her name was Olivia."

The hurricane of pain throbbing in John's head blew up to a category four. "You talked to her?"

"Uh-huh."

An arsenal of emotion assaulted him, one bullet at a time. Disbelief, incredulity—and a sudden undeniable wave of concern for a woman who should mean nothing to him. "Are you…what did she say?"

"That she was here for the reunion. And that she knew you."

"Why was she crying?"

"I don't know. But I think I made her feel a little better."

Soapsuds dripped from John's hands onto the spotless kitchen floor.

"Are you okay, Daddy? You look funny."

He took Flora's dishes and put them in the sink, a little too fast so that the edges clinked together. "Get your stuff, sweet pea, or you're gonna miss the bus."

For the next half hour, John put his brain on autopilot. He drove his daughter to the end of the driveway and waited with her until she had climbed on board and had sat down in the same seat she sat in every day, second row by the window.

He kept a rein on his feelings until the bus pulled away. He headed in the opposite direction toward town to do the weekly run for bag feed. A dozen different emotions raged through him. He did not, repeat *not,* want to think about Liv crying last night!

The only emotion he could deal with where she was concerned was anger. And he had every right in the world to be angry! What made her think she could just saunter back into town, show up at his farm bold as daylight and strike up a conversation with his daughter?

His anger at Liv was comfortable, like boots with a couple years' wear on them. But edging it out was something else. All the way to town, his daughter's voice kept penetrating the haze: *She was crying.*

He had seen Liv Ashford cry twice in his life. Once, in school, when her math teacher had died of leukemia. And another time when a stray puppy she'd been secretly taking care of in an old shed near her house had been hit by a car while meeting her at the school bus one afternoon.

Both times, seeing her with tears sliding down her cheeks, despite her efforts to hold them back, had torn him up inside. Both times, he'd pulled her in his arms and held her, wanting to absorb her pain, take it as his own so she no longer felt it.

The feelings came back now, strong and clear. He'd been a seventeen-year-old boy, and there was nothing more he'd wanted in the world than to spend his life making sure she never had a reason to cry.

She was crying.

Why?

The question wouldn't leave him alone.

John forced himself to heed the speed limit all the way into Summerville, even though he itched to take his frustration out on the accelerator beneath his foot.

Ahead on his right hung the big white sign for Dickson's Feed. Dickson's had been a fixture in Summerville for the past forty years, and the old brick building with its clay tile roof had once served as a train depot.

John swung the truck into the parking lot, the tires spitting gravel behind him. He backed up to the loading dock, revving the engine a little louder than he needed to, got out, slammed the door and took the back stairs three at a time. His boots thumped loudly on the dusty old wood floor of the warehouse.

Otis Olinger was stacking feed bags against a sidewall. He'd been working at Dickson's for as long as John could remember. A stiff wind would have blown Otis into the next county, every bag a small battle between him and the fifty-pound sacks. At the sight of John, he stopped, wiped a hand across an overheated brow and said, "Hey, John, you're never gonna guess—"

"Hey, Oat." John marched on through the warehouse. "I'm a little short on time today. Catch ya later, okay?"

"But John—" He didn't hear the rest of whatever it was Otis had been about to say. Because holding court in the center of the feed store's front room was Liv Ashford and two reporters from the *County Times*.

John stopped short as if he'd just run head on into a rock wall, his attention nailed to Liv's face. She was smiling. And for an instant he was glad because he couldn't seem to shake the image of her crying. He had forgotten how a smile transformed her. Or maybe he had refused to remember, and wasn't that a lot different from forgetting? She had on one of those summery outfits women wear, a sleeveless top and shorts the color of green grapes. Her arms and legs were lean and fit, the muscles long and defined. His pulse kicked up a few beats; attraction surged through him, as unwelcome as it was undeniable.

"Well, this oughta be a little extra seasoning for

your story, boys.'' The voice gave John a jolt. It was Harvey Dickson, the store owner, standing next to Liv, wearing a grin wider than that of most million-dollar lottery winners. The squash-colored CATERPILLAR hat on his head had two big grease stains on either side of the C and R. His overalls were due for a run through the washing machine, but the two-inch gaps between his cuffs and his well worn boots showed a strip of bleach-white socks. He was holding an introductory arm out in John's direction like a game-show hostess pointing out the next car up for giveaway. ''John here's Olivia's old beau. 'Livia worked here in high school. She told you that, though. Soon as John discovered that he was in here practically every day buyin' something for those horses. Got in a heap of trouble with his daddy for running up their charge account every month.'' This speech was followed up by a knowing chuckle.

The two reporters grinned. One had a ponytail longer than Flora's and a fan of gold studs in his left ear. The other wore khaki shorts and hiking boots that looked as though they'd never seen the dust of a trail.

As for Liv, all the color had drained from her face. And she wasn't smiling anymore.

John felt as if someone had dropped a big weight on his chest, and for the life of him, he couldn't move it.

The ponytailed reporter said, "Hey, could we get a shot of you two talking over there by the register? This'll be great! Like first loves seeing each other again for the—"

"Absolutely not!"

"I don't think so."

The first refusal came from Liv. The second from John. They were said in unison, with equal fervor.

Silence, stiff as new leather, got a stranglehold on the group, and they all stood there, frozen, as if someone had zapped them with a big pause button.

John broke the moment, backing up and heading for the door. "Put that feed on my tab, Harvey," he threw out. "I'll load it up myself."

IF ONLY THE FLOOR beneath her would just open up. Olivia tried to speak, but couldn't.

Coming here had been a bad idea. Lori had called this morning to confirm that she'd be coming for lunch and Olivia had decided to spend a couple hours in town looking around before heading to Lori's. Spur of the moment, she'd decided to drop in at Dickson's and say hello.

Across from her, Harvey shook his head with a see-I-know-what-I'm-talking-about look on his face. "Some things never change," he said. "You always could get that boy worked up."

The two reporters he'd called at the sight of Olivia—"you don't mind, do you? A store can't *buy* this kind of advertising!''—were looking as if they'd just had the plug pulled to a best-selling lead.

''I really have to be going, Mr. Dickson,'' Olivia said, suddenly feeling there wasn't enough air in the old store. ''It was really good to see you.''

''Well, you too, Olivia,'' he said. ''Now don't be a stranger.''

Despite her eagerness to leave, Olivia tried to make her exit look as casual as she could. Not that she imagined for a minute she'd succeeded.

As fate would have it—or maybe it was just sheer bad luck—the truck parked a few yards from her car belonged to John. And he was standing on the edge of the loading dock, throwing bags of horse feed onto the long bed at an Olympic-relay pace. Adrenaline poured through her. Her legs began to shake as if she'd just downed a few shots of espresso.

She intended to keep walking. The problem was her feet weren't following the directions from her brain. But the sight of him, while she stood there grounded, did not go unappreciated. With each bag he hefted and threw, a navy polo-type shirt strained at the width of his shoulders. And they were nice shoulders, broad like those of a man who used them daily, for work, not play.

To get to her own car, she had to walk right by him, which meant she had to make her legs move. Plus find the ability to speak—ironic considering articulation in awkward moments was part of the reason a major network paid her an exorbitant salary every year. But not one word came to mind now. She had somehow become both immobile and mute.

She pulled the remote from her pocket and aimed it at the car door. The beep sounded doubly obnoxious with John slinging feed bags in her peripheral vision.

"You locked your doors at Dickson's?"

His voice sent another jolt of surprise pounding along her nerve endings. So he had actually decided to acknowledge her presence. Maybe that could have meant something except that the derision coating the words was thick as peanut butter.

She forced an offended glare in his direction. "Habit."

"Oh, that's right. You're a city girl now."

There was nothing subtle about the jab, and the tone, as well as the words, hit her between the ribs. "So what exactly is the problem, John?" The question came out sounding breathless rather than disdainful—like she'd just run five miles. Uphill.

"No problem here." The pace of his feed-bag slinging accelerated. On the way to a world record now, for sure.

"I'm sorry if my being here this weekend is upsetting to you. But I have as much right to be here as anyone else. Unless they put you in charge of culling the guest list." Olivia had just given a perfect rendition of a pursed-lipped librarian.

He paused long enough to give her a steamy, somewhat disbelieving stare, as if he couldn't quite imagine such words coming from her mouth. He continued with his slinging. Two more bags, and he stopped altogether, his face set. "I don't appreciate you talking to my daughter behind my back."

So that's what this was all about. It took her a few seconds to find a response. "That was an accident."

"I'm not sure what that means, but how it happened doesn't matter. I don't want it to happen again."

A pickup truck pulled into the parking lot, the muffler loud and rusty-sounding. The plates said, Farm Use. It rumbled to a stop in the spot beside John. A man got out, his face and arms brown and sun-toughened. He threw up a hand. "Hey, John. Been meaning to call you on that orchard-grass hay. I could use about five hundred square bales this time. Think you'll have that much to spare?"

"Should be able to fix you up. Looks like we're gonna get a nice second cutting as long as things don't get too dry."

Olivia watched the exchange as if she were viewing it from behind one of those glass partitions like they use on cop shows: she could see them but they couldn't see her. John's whole demeanor had changed, the look on his face friendly, likable. With her, he'd been as unyielding as the concrete sidewalk beneath her feet. The transformation now made her ache for a time when the sight of her had brought light to his eyes and gladness to his face. Much as it had amazed her, even then.

"Sounds good," the man said to John, dropping a curious nod at Olivia, then heading up the steps and into the store.

A couple of cars rolled by on the street just out from the parking lot. One had the window rolled down and the base notes of some rap tune kept time with the thumping of Olivia's heart. Between John and her, a stretch of silence hung large and awkward like the wash on an old clothesline, weighed down in the middle.

"I'm really sorry about your wife, John," Olivia said now, the words coming out in a rush, almost before she'd realized her intent to say them.

He looked as if she'd just hit him with a bucket of ice water. He glanced down at the ground, his voice hoarse when he finally said, "When something that bad happens to someone that good, it's not easy to accept."

Olivia's heart hurt with the words, for the woman whose life had ended too soon, for the husband and daughter she had left behind, and selfish though it was, for the love he had obviously felt for her.

The air between them had changed for the moment, like a sudden break in a brewing storm.

"I don't think we ever realize our humanity more

than when we can't fix the bad things that happen to people we love,'' she said softly.

''It's a hard lesson,'' he said, shoving his hands in his pockets and kicking at the gravel beneath his boot. ''Figuring out that for the most part, we really aren't in control of anything. At least not the big stuff.''

''You really believe that?''

He looked up and met her gaze head on. ''Yeah, I really do.''

''You didn't used to look at life that way.''

He laughed, a short, disillusion-filled laugh. ''Yeah, well, I guess that's what growing up and becoming an adult really means.''

''Is that what you'll teach your daughter?''

Surprise widened his eyes. He started to say something, stopped, then gave her a long, steady look. ''I wouldn't do that to her childhood.''

Olivia folded her arms across her chest. She found it impossible to reconcile the John from her youth with this John. The John she had known at seventeen had been the first person ever to tell her she could do anything she wanted with her life. And to her that had been meaningful. *The world is open to you, Liv. You have everything it takes to be anything you want. It's all inside you. All you have to do is let it out.* She heard the words clearly now, remembered one night when they'd been out to a movie Olivia had loved, and she'd confessed to him her secret desire to write. When she was a girl, she'd kept journals, filling the pages with made-up stories and fragments of her own life as well. She'd been thirteen years old when her father had found a story she'd written about some kittens she'd discovered under an old house near where they lived. He'd had the pages in his hand one afternoon when she'd come home from school, and for one buoyant moment, she'd been sure he was going to tell her how much he liked it. Instead, he'd flung the pages across the floor and told her she'd never make straight As in school if she spent all her time going on about sentimental junk like that.

Olivia had stopped writing her short stories.

And so, the night John had told her she could be anything she wanted to be, she'd wanted to believe him. That was the John she'd missed so terribly over the years. But the man standing in front of her now bore little resemblance to that boy.

"So why exactly *did* you come back here?" John leveled at her now, his face again an unreadable mask. "I can't imagine there would be anything in Summerville of interest to you."

"This used to be my home, too."

"You didn't seem to have any trouble forgetting that," he said.

The storm was back.

It was stunning to discover how quickly her self-proclaimed indifference could collapse beneath the sting of his words. "Things aren't always exactly what they seem, John."

He took a step back. She'd surprised him. That much was clear.

Olivia clamped her mouth shut. Enough. Standing there in the middle of the Dickson's Feed parking lot, where memories of John were piled high like cast-aside hand-me-downs, anger seeped up inside her.

John thought he had the corner on the right to be furious over something she had done to him. The irony of that was almost more than she could hold inside another second longer. *She* had done to *him*. *She* was the one who'd had all choice taken away from her. Who'd been swept along on the consequences of someone else's behavior. *She* was the one still paying for those consequences today.

He thought she had run off to make a better life for herself and despised her for that. How would she feel if he knew the actual truth?

She'd come here wanting to put the past to rest. But standing in front of him now, she could not bring herself to say the words. To explain. To ask for forgiveness. The truth could only result in one thing. John would only end up blaming her as much as she blamed herself.

JOHN KEPT TO the speed limit on the drive back to Rolling Hills. For one crazy instant back there, he'd wanted to go after Liv and ask her what she'd meant by that remark. *Things aren't always exactly what they seem.*

As far as the two of them were concerned, things seemed pretty clear to him.

She was sorry about Laura. He'd hardly known what to say to that or how to respond. How could he talk to her about Laura? This woman he hadn't seen in fifteen years had been the one shadow in his marriage. Liv was the woman he had never forgotten, never gotten over, never stopped dreaming about at night when his unconscious mind took over and left him unable to shrug off the wants of his own heart. How could he talk to Liv about Laura when there were still moments he felt as if he might choke on the guilt of that?

But for a few moments, when Liv had looked at him with sympathy in her eyes, he'd felt a connection between them, a bond of empathy and a once-complete knowledge of who the other one was, what they were made of. No matter how much he might like his assessments of Liv Ashford to be true—a woman who'd decided there were bigger things in the world for her than him—he'd seen a glimpse of the Liv he had known fifteen years ago.

And it shook him to his center.

Since the moment he'd discovered she was back in Summerville, the anger inside him had been on autopilot, taking him where it would. He didn't like what he was seeing in himself. Or what his anger said to the world about his respect for the woman who had loved him the way most men would be grateful to have been loved.

Laura deserved so much better than that.

The truth was she had deserved a hell of a lot better than him.

And a hell of a lot better than the illness that had taken the life from her.

With the thought, grief and guilt struck up inside him, like the sudden clanging of brass instruments, the sound in his head a stark contrast to the peaceful silence around him.

He'd failed his wife in many ways. But the failure that loomed largest was his inability to love her as a wife deserved to be loved by her husband. Because the truth was with Liv he'd found the other side of himself. Knew that she was meant for him. With Liv there had been a click, a fit, a deep satisfaction of knowing they'd been made for one another—he'd believed that with all his heart, with an almost arrogant certainty that they would spend the rest of their lives together.

But then Liv had left, and he'd felt as if someone had let the air out of his life, leaving him flat, empty, torn up with the kind of hurt a person didn't get over.

And he hadn't gotten over it.

This was the part he'd never admitted to himself

until now. After she'd left, he'd gone on with his life as a man must who has accepted the end of a relationship that turned out not to be what he'd thought it was. But the truth was he'd closed down a part of himself after that, simply locked it up, hung a big Access Denied sign out front.

And he'd never let Laura in, never loved her with the freedom that can only come from an unscarred heart.

This, he regretted.

This, he would change if he could. But it wasn't in his power to change the past. The only thing he could affect was the here and now. Being angry at Liv said things he did not want said. A man with indifference in his heart didn't act the way he'd been acting.

At the barn, John backed the truck up to the feed-room door, got out and started unloading the bags of grain. He'd just reached for the last bag, hefted it onto his shoulder when Sophia walked up.

"Hot work," she said, handing him a glass of lemonade. "Thought you could use this."

John took the glass, wiped his cheek on the shoulder of his shirt and said, "Thanks. It's a little warm out here."

Sophia hesitated, shuffled from one foot to the other, then reached in her apron pocket and pulled out a plain white envelope. She held it out to him.

"I have no idea if now's the time for this or not, John. It feels like it might be, so I hope I'm right."

He reached for the envelope, glanced at the front and recognized Laura's handwriting. Alarm jolted through him. "What is it?"

"I haven't read it," she said, her expression serious in a way he rarely saw it. "Before she died, she asked me to give it to you when I thought you might be ready to make another life for yourself. I don't know if you are or not, son. But it's time you did." She thwacked him on the shoulder, the gesture awkward, affectionate, and he could see tears in her eyes now. "I'll be in the house if you need me."

She left him standing there then, the envelope pressed between his thumb and forefinger like some foreign object he wasn't even sure how to hold, much less what to do with.

A red bird flitted by, landed on a nearby white azalea, sang a note or two, then flew off again. John stood frozen to the spot. The screen door at the back of the house wheezed open, then flapped closed, the sound reverberating through him.

He looked down at the envelope. Part of him wanted to know what was inside, but another part did not.

He stuck it in his pocket, went in the barn and got Eli out of his stall. He snapped a single-tie to the halter of the two-year-old gelding, squirted him with some fly spray, then saddled him up and led him out of the barn. Despite the warm weather, the young horse was full of himself, doing his best to jig all the way out the gravel road leading away from the barn.

They passed a field lush with orchard grass. Eli balked a little, wanting to stop and graze. John urged him on, and they soon left the tempting field behind, following an old dirt road that led to the hills on the backside of the farm. By the time they reached the top, Eli was sweating, and John's shirt was sticking to his back. He got off, led the horse to the creek and let him have a short drink.

The temperature was just slightly cooler up here, the soft stirring of air a welcome relief from the June sun that had beat down on them most of the way up. An oak tree threw shade across the spot. John sat down on the trunk of a maple that had fallen last winter during an ice storm. He looped the reins on the jut of a broken limb and let the gelding nibble at the grass growing along the edge of the creek bank.

It was cool and peaceful here, this place John had come to often in his life, maybe his favorite on the farm. He wasn't sure he ever came consciously, but he always seemed to wind up here whenever he had something going on inside him that needed consideration. When he was younger, it was here where he'd always seemed able to put a label on things, figure out how to fix them. As an adult, that hadn't

always proven true. Not with Liv. And not with
Laura.

He pulled the envelope out of his pocket and
stared at it a full minute before turning it over and
slitting the top open. He slipped the paper out, unfolded it with a good amount of trepidation and began to read.

John,

I hope this letter finds you at a very different
place from where you've been these last few
months. I know this isn't where any of us
thought life would take us. At least not so soon.
And I'm sorry for it, for you, me, Flora, all of
us. But this is what is. And I have faced it,
made peace with it.

Thank you for being here for me, for taking
care of me, for loving me. I know that you
have. I don't think we've loved each other in
exactly the same ways, but it's all right. It's
been more than enough, John. I want you to
know that.

There are so many things I wish I had the
courage to say to you face to face. But I'm
selfish, I guess, and although I want to clear
my conscience of what I am about to tell you,
I can't face the possibility that you might hate
me for it.

A month or so after we were married and

moved back to the farm, a girl came to see you. You and your father were away that weekend, and I answered the door. She asked for you. I told her you weren't here, but that I was your wife and could I help her? She was shocked by what I'd said. She had walked to the house, and I regret that I didn't at the least offer her a ride somewhere. I'd like to think I was under the influence of jealousy and fear of losing you. But even that doesn't excuse what I did.

I just didn't want her ever to come back. I wanted our life to go on as it was, commuting back and forth to school, living at Rolling Hills. I loved our life so much. I might not have known everything, but I knew that before we met, someone had hurt you terribly, and as soon as I saw her, I knew she was the one. It wasn't until much later, after I found those letters, that I realized exactly what you two had meant to one another.

I wish now that I had told you, given you the chance to make a choice. But in all honesty, I'm not sure I would do anything differently. Because to do so might have meant losing you and never having Flora. And I don't think I could ever be that selfless.

John, it's only natural that you will grieve when I am gone. We had a lot of years together, and though I was never the woman of your heart, I know you loved me in your own way. I will ask Sophia to give you this when she thinks you are ready to read it. I want to set you free now if I can. You have been a wonderful husband and an incredible father. And I know that Flora will grow up to be something special because of you. Remember me as someone who loved you, but go on now, John. Live the rest of your life. Make it rich and full, without regrets. And know that I loved you, our daughter and our life together.

Laura

His hand let go of the letter. It fell to his side.

His wife's voice echoed from the pages, and the first thing he felt was a well of sadness so deep it couldn't possibly have a bottom. Laura. Lord, life was unfair. Whatever had brought them together, kept them together, the world was less without her in it.

His heart throbbed. He didn't fight it, didn't try to push it away, but instead let the pain play out, absorbing at the same time, the realization that Liv had come back all those years ago.

Laura had been afraid to tell him.

Liv had come back.

Why?

And how could Laura not have told him?

He let that question take root and waited to see if

anger would rise up. How could he blame Laura for what she had done?

The truth was, he couldn't.

They had married fast. Some had said too fast. And when they'd met during those first months at the University of Virginia, he had been in such a fog that he wasn't sure what his exact reasons for asking her to marry him were. He just knew they'd had something to do with trying to find a way to pull the plug on the awful hurt that had not subsided in him since Liv had left Summerville. He had never intended to hurt Laura. He knew that much. He'd been too young and too green to see far enough ahead to realize all the ramifications of an impulsiveness that had been based on his own selfish desire to forget Liv.

But even now, from a perspective shaped by fifteen years of separate lives and a good woman who had loved him, he couldn't say that he would not have changed his life had he been here the day she had knocked on his door.

He picked up the letter, looked at the familiar handwriting again.

God help him, he should be able to, but he couldn't say it.

CHAPTER SEVEN

Comparisons

OLIVIA TOOK HER TIME driving out to Lori's, leaving the town limits and heading out into the county, stretches of rain-blessed cornfields blending into hay fields ready for the next cutting. On the left just ahead was a country store with white clapboard and a red tin roof and two gray-haired men on a bench out front quenching their thirst with small-bottle Cokes.

Wired with a thousand different feelings, Olivia wasn't sure which to tackle first. Her cheeks still burned from the scene with John at the feed store. *He can only hurt you if you let him, Olivia.*

Two more days and she would be gone. They would never see each other again. She lifted her right hand from the wheel. It was still shaking.

One thing was clear. John could barely stand the sight of her.

She blinked, trying to focus on the Virginia countryside rolling by. She knew this road well. The old house where she'd grown up sat off this road, the turn just ahead on the right. She glanced in her rearview mirror. No cars behind her. She let up on the accelerator, her heart doubling its rhythm. The gravel road was still there, although vines and bushes had narrowed it to little more than a car's width.

Should she go look? See if the old house was still standing?

But then what was the point? There was nothing there but memories whose edges had at least been dulled, if not obliterated, with time and distance.

What good would come from seeing the old house again?

Olivia pressed the accelerator to the floor, leaving the driveway behind and letting the BMW flirt with the upper end of the speed limit.

Her phone rang. Caller ID showed Michael's cell number.

"Hey. Just wondering if you were having a good time."

"Yes," she said, not elaborating. "In fact, are you sure you want to come all the way down here? Not obligatory."

"You went with me to that bore-you-to-tears black-tie thing a few weeks ago. I owe you."

"Where are you?"

"Actually, I'm still in the city. We've got a big meeting scheduled for tomorrow morning. Last-minute. Appearance mandatory. Would it be a very big deal if I didn't come until the afternoon?''

"No," she said. "You really don't have to come at all, Michael. Being dateless won't kill me."

"There are two places where showing up without a date is like twin root canals: Weddings and reunions," he said, a smile in his voice.

She let it go then and refused to ask herself if letting Michael off the hook had anything to do with John. "I'll see you tomorrow."

Just ahead, a small green sign—Gibson Road— marked the turn to Lori's house. Olivia followed the tree-lined road a half-mile or so, and there at the end was an all-American setting—a house very much like the house Lori had grown up in and exactly what she'd always said she wanted. It was old, maybe turn-of-the-century, a white two-story with large windows and dark green shutters. It had recently been repainted. The front porch held two hanging swings, both of which were currently occupied by four children, three with dark hair like Sam's, one with red like Lori's. Each of them could have been in an advertisement for Gap Kids. They were every bit as beautiful as Lori had described them.

Olivia stopped her car under a tree heavy with green apples. At the sight of her, the children all clamored out of the swings and scrambled into the house, yelling, "Mama, mama, somebody's here!"

Olivia got out of the car, feeling as out of place as a piece of contemporary furniture in the middle of a room done in American country. A flagstone sidewalk led to the front-porch steps. The door swung open again, and Sam stepped outside, a smile on his face. "Hey, Olivia."

"Hi, Sam. I don't think I've ever seen prettier children."

"We're a little prejudiced, but we've decided to keep them." His smile widened. "Come on in. Lori's just upstairs putting on the finishing touches. She said to send you up. Second room on the left."

"Okay, thanks."

Like the outside, Lori's was the kind of house that felt lived in, the walls done in soothing earth tones of gold and cinnamon and taupe. Olivia went upstairs, stopping at a bedroom where Lori sat at a vanity running a brush through her hair, four children under the age of seven anchored to her sides with what looked like a sudden bout of shyness. Emotion capsized inside Olivia. Wistfulness? Envy?

"Hi," Lori said, catching sight of Olivia in the mirror and smiling. "I'm so glad you're here."

"Me, too." Olivia tipped a shoulder against the doorframe.

"Let me introduce you." Lori pointed, starting with the smallest child. "Christopher, Mark, Rachel and Ashley. Say hello to Miss Ashford."

"Hi." "Hewwo," came a chorus of curious greetings.

"Hello," Olivia said. "It's very nice to meet all of you."

"Would you guys mind letting Mommy have a minute to talk with Olivia? How about if you go on downstairs with Daddy? We'll be down in a few minutes and make some lunch."

They filed out of the bedroom, their footsteps reluctant. At the top of the stairs, they thundered down in a race to see who would get to the bottom first.

"They're adorable."

Lori smiled. "Thank you. Some days I don't know what to do with them, and others I don't know what I'd do without them."

"You're obviously doing something right. They look like very happy children."

"That's the ultimate compliment to me," she said. "Raising children is the most difficult thing I've ever done. There's no manual, no handbook, no four-year degree. So many nights I go to bed wondering if I should have handled something differently."

"But you had such a good go-by," Olivia said. "Your parents probably taught you more than you'll ever realize about doing the right thing."

"Here, sit down." Lori patted the chair beside her vanity. "I hope I didn't sound like a total cornball last night when I was talking about what's important to me these days.''

"I assure you that's the last thing I thought." Olivia looked down, adding, ''Actually, I was more than a little jealous.''

Lori could not have looked more surprised. ''With the life you have? How could you be jealous of me?''

Olivia met her friend's disbelieving gaze. "I don't have what you have," she said, feeling the truth of her own words even as she said them. In this house, her own life felt suddenly thin.

"But Olivia, your life must be so glamorous and exciting! All those beautiful clothes you wear, getting to look like a million dollars all the time! I can only imagine.''

"They're just clothes," Olivia said. And then, surprising herself, added, ''Sometimes I feel like it doesn't really matter whether it's me sitting in front of the camera or not. It's as if that's just this person I've created to do the job, and there's not much of the real me showing through.''

Lori looked startled by the confession. ''Is it something you want to keep doing?''

"I always thought so. Oh, don't get me wrong. I hope I'm not sounding ungrateful. I've been given some wonderful opportunities.''

"Can I ask you a personal question?''

"Of course.''

"Why haven't you ever gotten married?"

Olivia shrugged with what she hoped passed as nonchalance. "I think I just ended up not being the marrying kind."

"You were once," Lori said pointedly. And then with a smile, "Back when you were John Riley's girl."

Just the words made Olivia's chest tighten and ache. There had been a time when that was all she wanted to be. "That was a long time ago."

"But you're still the same person."

"In some ways. In most ways, I think I'm very different. And most of the time, I'm pretty happy with the way things are," Olivia said, but the words did not sound convincing.

"I always pictured you with children. You and John. It was just one of those things I couldn't imagine being any other way."

"How can you really know what you want at that age?" Olivia managed, and even to her ears, her voice did not sound like her own.

"Some things, I think you just know." Lori picked up a pot of foundation and ran her thumb across the top. "John is a proud man. Maybe you didn't realize what it did to him when you left."

The words held no trace of criticism, but all the same, Olivia heard the conviction behind them. "We were teenagers, Lori. He moved on pretty quickly."

This time, it was Lori who seemed to have trouble finding words. She put the lid back on her makeup. Picked up a hairbrush. Put it back down. "I don't really feel comfortable talking about this with everything that's happened, but there were a lot of rumors floating around when he married Laura. A lot of people thought he married her to get over you."

The words hit like hammer strikes against some soft, vulnerable spot deep inside Olivia. She swallowed, then blinked hard. Was it possible that he had *not* gotten over her so quickly? That all this time she might have been wrong in thinking that his heart had never ached for her even a little?

"Losing you changed him. He grew up overnight. He got serious about life. It was like he didn't have the heart to be young and frivolous. He didn't hang out with the rest of us anymore."

Olivia had no idea what to say. All these years, she had pictured something so entirely different. Imagined that John had met Laura, fallen head over heels in love with her and forgotten that he'd ever known Olivia. The possibility that it might not have happened exactly that way lit a flame in her heart, a gentle *whoof* of hope, unsummoned, maybe even unwelcome, but there, nonetheless. "I saw him earlier over at Dickson's," she said, her voice again a rusty replica of itself.

"And let me guess, he wasn't wearing his welcome hat?"

That, at least, got a half smile out of Olivia. "It was actually pretty awful."

Lori sighed. "I have no idea whether the two of you will ever be friends, Olivia, but I do know John. He's a good man. People have different ways of showing hurt."

Olivia weighed her old friend's assertion. Was it possible that John's anger had begun with hurt? The thought brought with it implications she would never have considered under the chill of his gaze earlier that morning.

But she wondered on into the afternoon when they went downstairs to have lunch at the round maple table in the center of Lori's kitchen. Grilled cheese sandwiches for the children, a Caesar salad for the big folks. It was the loudest, messiest lunch she'd ever had as an adult. And it was also the best, one she knew she would remember for a long time to come. Because there at that table, in full, living color was exactly what was missing from her own life.

UNDER ORDINARY CIRCUMSTANCES, John was a ten-minute man. Five to shower, three to shave, one and a half to brush his teeth, a few seconds to comb his hair. Tonight, however, he'd broken all records, standing under the faucet until his skin started to shrivel and the hot water had lost its bravado.

The goose bumps finally won out, and he reached

for a towel, dried off and cracked the bathroom door to check on Flora who was sitting on his bed, a sketch pad on her lap and an assortment of crayons spread out around her. "You all right in there?"

"Mmm-hmm," she said without glancing up. John watched her for a moment and then smiled at the intensity on his daughter's face. She was into her crayons in a major way, and she loved to sit on his bed and draw while he got ready.

He thought maybe Flora felt closer to her mother in a room Laura had decorated with heavy yellow and rose floral drapes, a thick down comforter with matching duvet and chunky pillows atop a four-poster bed found at an estate auction in Wythe County. After Laura died, John had wanted to move out of the room, but that would have been one more change for Flora to accept along with everything else. He just hadn't had the heart to do it.

John finished shaving, swatted a comb across his hair and went into the bedroom for a shirt. He had changed three times and was about to go for another one when Flora said, "Daddy, why do you keep changing clothes?"

Halfway out of the shirt, John stopped, considered fudging the truth, then reminded himself he couldn't preach honesty as a virtue to his daughter if he didn't practice it himself. "It's called a delaying tactic, sweet pea."

"What's a d'laying tactic?" she asked without

lifting her gaze from the pad pinned beneath a red crayon.

"It's when you find reasons to put off doing something you don't want to do."

She looked up, her small face scrunched in a frown. "Like when I can't find my shoes because I don't want to go to school?"

"Like that."

"Oh. I like that shirt. Blue's my favorite color, you know."

"Then blue it is." He rebuttoned the shirt he'd been about to take off. Yesterday, her favorite color had been green, but he didn't bother to contradict her. It was a woman's prerogative to change her mind. He wasn't about to discourage it.

At seven, Flora was a walking encyclopedia of questions. *Daddy, why do cows lie down when it rains? Daddy, why are stop signs red?* She'd thrown him some stumpers, that was for sure. But it was also one of his favorite parts of being a father, trying to find answers for his daughter, even when he didn't always have them for himself.

He glanced at his watch. It was seven-thirty, and he had thought of at least a thousand excuses not to go tonight, some of them pretty good, too. But none of them held water under scrutiny of any duration. And as soon as Cleeve got here, he'd be dragging him out of the house by his blue shirt collar, anyway.

Through the open bedroom window, John could already hear the music thumping out its bass beat, keeping pretty good rhythm with the headache he'd tossed a couple Advil at that afternoon and still hadn't managed to shake.

"Daddy?"

"What, sweet pea?" Just the tone told him there was a doozy coming.

"Are you ever going to go out on a date?"

John stared at his daughter's reflection in the bathroom mirror, then swung around to face her, the razor he'd been about to put back in the wall cabinet falling from his hand and making a loud, clattering noise in the sink. "What?"

"Sammy Sullivan said daddies never went this long without dating, and that it wasn't normal."

"And how did seven-year-old Sammy Sullivan claim to know such a thing?"

"He said his mama was talking about you, and that's what she said."

Red rage went over him in a wave, and he wished he could round up all the busybodies in this town and put them on a bus to somewhere where they could meddle in somebody's business who didn't mind. He minded. "Sometimes people talk about things they have no business talking about," he said, careful not to let his irritation show.

"But will you?"

John looked at his daughter then, and saw the

confusion on her face. He should have known there was something other than idle curiosity behind her question. He went over to the bed, moved aside a few crayons and pulled her onto his lap. "I don't know the answer to that. But I do know one thing. Your mama will never be replaced. Other people might come into our lives, but they'll never replace her. Do you understand?"

Flora laid her head against his chest and looked down at her lap. "I still miss her, Daddy."

"I know you do, baby. So do I. And that's a good thing because it reminds us how important she was to us. She'd want us to miss her, but she wouldn't want us to be sad too long."

"Are you still sad?"

Laura's words from the letter he'd read that afternoon floated up. "A part of me always will be. But it would make your mama sad if we didn't try to be happy without her."

"Aunt Sophia says you've gotta deal with your regret before you can ever be happy again."

"And how do you know Sophia said that?" he asked, shaking his head.

"That's what she told Uncle Hank. What's regret?"

"Sadness for things you didn't do, baby."

"Do you have lots of regrets, Daddy?"

"Not too many," he said. And then, "A few."

"How do you make them go away?"

"I don't know." He pulled his daughter into the curve of his arm and hugged her tight. "I wish I did."

A LITTLE WHILE LATER, John made his way out to the front yard of the house where the second night of reunion festivities was now in full swing. There was a DJ tonight, and the music was loud. It would get louder as the night wore on, he was sure. No one was dancing. Too early, he supposed. Not enough cocktails dealt out by the bartender yet to turn inhibition into courage.

He got himself a Coke and ended up in a corner of the yard next to a potted fig tree that looked about as conspicuous as he felt.

The moment she arrived, John knew it. His face went warm, and his hands started to tingle. He looked up at the front table just as every head in the crowd swiveled in the same direction.

People flowed toward her, then clustered around her. She smiled, was more than polite, but she wasn't comfortable with the attention. He could see that from here, even with fifty yards and fifteen years between them. It was there in the rigid way she held her shoulders, the way her hand kept fluttering to the base of her throat.

John tried to look elsewhere, but his own gaze betrayed him, and he found himself taking a good long look at her. She'd worn green again tonight. A sleeveless sweater with a rounded neck and skinny black pants. Her hair was loose, just barely glancing her shoulders.

She disappeared into the crowd, but the sight of her lifted a memory to the surface. Liv with a ponytail. It had been longer then. And sun-lightened. They'd been sitting on the grass beneath the very same oak tree under which she now stood. It was springtime, early May, and they were supposed to be doing calculus homework, but with Liv on his lap, her head on his shoulder, there had been no way he could keep his mind on anything that boring. He remembered her clothes: cut-off Levi's, a white tank top with skinny straps and yellow flip-flops, the kind you got at the drugstore for ninety-nine cents. Her arms and legs were smooth and tan from Saturday afternoons spent on the dock at the pond behind his house. He remembered pulling the rubber band out of her hair, the way the long strands had fallen across her shoulders, spilling over his hands, the sensation the most sensual he'd ever known.

And he also remembered now, as clearly as he'd ever remembered anything, the feeling he'd had that afternoon. His sense of absolute completeness, fulfillment, the undeniable rightness of his love for her. He had thought they were forever. Eighteen years old, and he'd been totally certain that if he never achieved another thing in his life, finding Liv would be enough.

She'd come back to see him all those years ago. She'd come back, and he'd never known.

The knowledge left him feeling like a sailboat without a rudder, and just the simple act of keeping himself upright took all his concentration.

He looked around for Cleeve, but didn't see him.

Needing a few minutes away from the crowd, he headed down to the barn to check on Nadine. She'd thrown a shoe that afternoon and was confined to her stall tonight because the farrier couldn't come until the morning. The other horses were all out, except for Popcorn, whom he'd left in to keep the filly company.

He let himself in the barn's side door, not bothering to flick on the aisle lights. The moon would cast enough shadow through the open Dutch doors for him to see the two horses and throw them some hay if they needed it.

He heard her before he saw her. That voice was unmistakable. He stood there in the center of the darkened aisle with his feet bolted to the floor, unable to move while something heavy and a little painful settled in his chest.

This voice was familiar, one he remembered, thought he'd forgotten and realized now that he hadn't. This wasn't the one she had cultivated for her TV audience. That voice belonged to a woman he did not know. This belonged to a girl he had once thought he'd known better than he knew himself.

He followed the sound.

Naddie's stall door was slightly open. And there was Liv, standing inside with her forehead tipped against the filly's mane, smoothing a hand across her neck and speaking to her in that voice women reserve for babies and animals, soft and crooning. The filly was nosing around her pockets, looking for carrots the same way she did with Flora.

John couldn't make his voice work.

Liv looked up, starting at the sight of him. Naddie jumped, saw it was only him and went back to her carrot search.

"John, I...you scared me," Liv said, her eyes wide.

"Sorry." He folded his arms across his chest as if planting them there would make his heart stop beating so hard.

"Actually, I guess I shouldn't be in here. I was just..." She threw a hand back toward the party. "I kind of wanted to get away for a few minutes. Regroup. Is True still here?"

The question flashed before him an image of Liv cantering bareback and bridleless on the old quarter horse he'd learned to ride on and had taught her on as well when they'd first started dating in the spring of their junior year in high school.

"He died a few years ago," he said, swallowing hard.

Sadness washed across her face. "Oh. I'm sorry.

I guess he would have been pretty old by now. I know you must miss him.''

The words went straight to the core of him. Maybe because he knew she had loved that horse as much as he had, spoiling him with carrots and apples so that it got to the point that every time she walked in the barn, True knocked on the stall door with a front hoof until she came back to see him, treats in tow.

She stepped out of the stall now, giving Naddie a last rub on the neck. John slid the door closed behind her and hooked the latch.

They stood there in the aisle, moonshadows lighting their faces. Popcorn moved in his stall and rattled his feed bucket, no doubt looking for a last morsel of grain left over from dinner. Neither John nor Olivia said a thing, the silence between them so awkward that he didn't know how to begin to tackle it.

"I probably shouldn't have come down here," she said, her voice startling in the quiet.

"Probably not," he agreed, although not for the reasons he would have given last night at this time. She was stirring up way too many memories. Things he thought he'd forgotten. Things he'd needed to forget and did *not* want to remember now.

Even in the half dark, he could see her face go a shade paler with his response. Something between satisfaction and regret stabbed through him, and there was nothing at all palatable in the combination. He felt mean like one of the boys on the playground who tried to yank Flora's pigtails at recess. He wanted to qualify what he'd said, but how did he qualify fifteen years worth of hurt without baring his soul, without reopening wounds that were still just beneath the surface, wounds that had never healed?

She stepped away from him then, the movement quick and awkward. She lost her balance and banged her shoulder on the stall door. His arm shot out to steady her. He caught himself just short of touching her, making for a couple of word-defying awkward seconds. He jerked his hand back as if someone had just lit a flame under it. And they stood there, two strangers who had once known one another's most intimate thoughts, with him thinking that there had been a time when he would have kissed that shoulder and made it better. In a moment frozen between then and now, he saw himself doing exactly that, imagined brushing his lips across the ridge of that shoulder, following line and curve to the spot just behind her left ear where he had discovered as a green seventeen-year-old boy that she had loved most to be kissed.

Did she still?

Want kicked up inside him, as overpowering as any need he had ever known. And although self-preservation shouted in his ear, he could not make himself look away. A piece of hay clung to her hair.

Sawdust speckled her pants and sandals. He reached out and brushed away the hay, the action so impulsive, that his intention never even registered until the gesture was complete.

He saw her quick intake of breath and realized she was as thrown by the lapse as he was.

"I owe you an apology for this morning."

That he had surprised her was clear. She started to speak, stopped, and then said, "It's all right."

"No. It wasn't."

Neither of them said anything for a string of moments, the silence full as if they were both trying to figure out where they stood with one another.

Oscar, one of the barn cats, hopped off his perch above Popcorn's stall door and sidled around Liv's legs. She squatted down, picked up the cat and rubbed the back of its neck. The cat purred with contentment. "I didn't come back here to hurt you, John," Liv said.

The John of this morning would have fired out a blustery denial of her ability to have any effect on him at all. But the John of tonight let it stand. "Liv. After you left that summer...I never knew you came back to see me."

She looked down at the concrete floor beneath their feet and tipped a sandaled foot on end, her hands fluttering a little as if it were information she didn't quite know what to do with. "That was a long time ago."

"Yeah, it was." A pocket of awkward silence hung between them, and then, "So why did you, Liv?"

She shook her head, then glanced up at him, her eyes meeting his, carefully shuttered of emotion. "It was a silly impulse."

"The same impulse that made you just decide to pick up your life and start it all over somewhere else without me?" It would have been nice to think he'd just asked that question with something close to indifference in his voice. He would have been kidding himself.

She met his gaze, a wounded look in her eyes. "All the way here, I kept telling myself that so many years had passed you would have forgotten all about me."

"How could I forget—" *Whoa, John. Wrong turn.* He backed up and tried another direction. "You're right. It was a long time ago. We were just kids."

"Mmm-hmm." She nodded.

Her lips parted as if she were about to say something, then made a seam beyond which the words couldn't pass.

"What was it you had to have, Liv, that I couldn't give you?"

It was a long time before she answered him. And finally, "Oh, John, it wasn't you."

"No. It sure wasn't." He took a couple of steps

back, certain that if he didn't leave now, he'd say something he would later have cause to regret. "Stay as long as you like, Liv. The horses always like the company."

CHAPTER EIGHT

Old Songs and Memories

ARE THERE JUST some people in the world whom we are destined to be hurt by again and again?

This was the question Olivia asked herself when John headed down the center aisle of the barn and out the big sliding doors.

For a few moments, they had reconnected. For a few brief seconds, something that had once been was again. It had not been the wistful yearnings of her imagination. She'd seen the shock of it on his face as well, the unexpected recognition of something he had not intended to feel.

Olivia stood there in the darkened barn trembling.

How many times had she told herself the feelings she'd had for John were those of another girl in another lifetime? They couldn't possibly exist in any form in the here and now. But it had taken no more than hearing that he had not forgotten what had once been between them to make a mockery of her own denials.

And in all honesty, had she truly eased him out of her heart all those years ago, she'd be able to stand in front of him now without that same vital organ thumping off rhythm as though it had forgotten a pattern it had managed perfectly well for thirty-three years.

Olivia gathered up her tattered composure and headed back to the front yard where the music had gotten louder and people had begun dancing. She'd barely reached the edge of the crowd when Cleeve Harper came at her with grinning intent, his smile white enough to get him his own toothpaste commercial. He rolled out a palm. "You look like you could use a little fun, ma'am. How about dancing with a rhythmless cowboy?"

"Oh, Cleeve, I don't know—"

"Come on," he said, taking her hand and leading her into the throng of dancers making use of the temporary wood floor set up on the grass, a speaker in each corner.

The DJ was playing a range of old stuff. Bruce Hornsby. Prince. George Michael. Songs Olivia rarely heard on the radio anymore, but the beat made her want to dance the way the music you listened to when you were young always does.

Cleeve kept Olivia's hand in his, twirled her around a time or two, took her by the waist and dipped her right, then left. Laughter bubbled past her lips when he set her straight again. "You're pretty good at this," she said.

"Why, that's mighty gracious of you, ma'am, but it's just the Harper way to figure out how to please a lady," he said, grinning at her from beneath the brim of the Stetson she'd yet to see him take off.

"So I've heard," she said.

His smile widened.

They danced to songs Olivia hadn't heard in years, and there was something about hearing them here in this setting that transported her back to the good memories. To Friday-night football games at the Summerville High stadium and sockhops afterward where she and John had danced to Duran Duran and Huey Lewis, while somewhere nearby Cleeve dipped and spun his latest crush. To Saturday nights in the Dairy Queen parking lot, sitting on the tailgate of John's truck, the AM radio blasting a fuzzy version of Fleetwood Mac through the truck's makeshift clothes-hanger antenna.

Cleeve was still a good dancer, light on his feet for a man his size. They bopped their way through at least ten songs, shagging to a couple, doing a few Travolta moves for the retro disco stuff. Olivia's top clung to her back, and her hair had grown damp at the sides and at her neck. And she laughed. With nothing but sheer enjoyment of the moment. Not caring if she looked silly, just having fun. And it felt so good, like a favorite place she hadn't been to in a very long time.

"Well, I'll be. Never thought I'd see that."

Olivia followed Cleeve's gaze to where John was being pulled onto the dance floor by an attractive woman with dark-brown hair. She tipped her head back and saw surprise on Cleeve's face. "What?"

"John dancing." He glanced that way again.

"He used to like to dance." The words were out before she ever realized her intention of saying them. "I mean—"

"Yep, he did."

Neither of them said anything for half a song.

"What made you leave here the way you did, Olivia?" Cleeve finally asked, the words coming out in a rush. "Without telling anyone, I mean?"

"It was complicated, Cleeve."

"I reckon it was, but you had some good friends here. It was kind of hard to understand why you would just up and run off that way."

Something about the earnestness in Cleeve's eyes made her want him to know it hadn't been her choice. All these years, and the people she had cared about here thought she'd decided there were better things out there for her than what this town had to offer. What else *could* they have thought? Another stanza of song played by before she found the words to say, "It wasn't something I ever intended to do,

Cleeve, and I missed everyone so much at times I thought I might actually die from it.''

He looked down at her, as serious as she'd ever seen him, and there was understanding in his eyes, despite her flimsy explanation. ''What you and John had then was something that doesn't come along all that often. Even an old farm boy like me could see that. It nearly tore him in half when you left here, Olivia.''

She chose her words carefully, wanted them to mean something, but felt even before she said them the lack of conviction behind them. ''We were little more than kids then, Cleeve. And I think at that age we just have a special talent for believing we feel things more deeply than the rest of the world.''

''Well, that may be. But I know what I saw. What you two had was the real thing. At least as real as I've ever seen.''

Cleeve braked them to a jolting halt in the middle of the dance floor. John and the woman dancing with him stood at a startled standstill beside them.

''Olivia, you remember Racine Delaney?'' Cleeve waved a hand between the two of them.

''Pagans Delaney,'' the woman said. ''Hello, Olivia.''

And then Olivia did remember, only the Racine of today barely resembled the Racine Pagans Olivia had known in high school. She remembered her as plain with thick glasses. The woman standing in front of her was beautiful.

"Hello, Racine," she said, trying not to show her surprise. "You look wonderful."

"Thank you," Racine said, looking startled by the compliment in the way of a woman who doesn't believe it true of herself.

"Y'all mind if we switch for a little while?" Cleeve's voice boomed near Olivia's ear, the tone as reasonable as if he'd just asked if he could get her a glass of iced tea.

Good manners carried on a silent but visible war across the planes of John's face.

Cleeve didn't bother waiting for an answer. He handed Olivia over to John, then whirled Racine off across the floor, her squeal of delight trailing behind like exhaust fumes.

"We don't have to do this," Olivia said, any poise she might have thought herself in possession of vanishing in a poof of awkwardness.

"We'd be a little conspicuous not to at this point."

He pulled her into his arms then, as if he'd made up his mind at that very second. She toppled forward into him. Air whooshed from her chest in a gasp. She followed his lead in a slow circle, her heart pounding in her ears. Surely he could hear it? She tried putting her thoughts in another place—what was the title of this song? Were those bushes at the corner of the house rhododendrons? Anything to dispel the awful embarrassment of knowing John would rather be anywhere else in the world than on this dance floor with her.

"You think he planned that?" she finally found the voice to ask.

"Knowing Cleeve? He's always been into outlaw justice." The words held tolerance instead of a reprimand.

"I guess knowing him as long as you have, you've had a lot of experience with it."

"Remember the time he lifted those English tests from Mrs. Smith's briefcase because he hadn't had time to study?"

Olivia smiled. "How many days did it take her to find them?"

"Three. Cleeve got an A+, and he'll swear to this day that he never looked at the questions."

Olivia laughed, surprising herself and John, as well, if the widening of his eyes was anything to go by. She should be angry with Cleeve, at the very least, outdone. But any anger she might have summoned collapsed altogether beneath the reality of circling this floor in John's arms, a place she had never imagined being again.

A couple behind them skirted by too close, and John pulled her in so that there was barely a hand's width between them. Olivia felt, suddenly, as if she had been sensitized to everything about him. The faint remnant of whatever soap he'd showered with earlier. The slight sheen of moisture on his neck at the opening of his shirt. The brush of stiff denim against the softer fabric of her linen pants. The awareness was both painful and pleasurable at once.

The song changed. Olivia was sure he would step back, let her go.

But he didn't.

He could have led her from the dance floor now. They'd danced one song. Maybe that had been necessary in order not to create a spectacle in front of a group of people who knew their history. But it would be hard to make that the rationale for the second song. If one were rationalizing, that was. In that moment, Olivia made a conscious decision not to.

The song playing was an old Bryan Adams song. Olivia froze for a moment, long enough to lose the rhythm of the music. John paused and let her catch the next beat without otherwise acknowledging she was off. It was the song that had thrown her. A song to which she had once known every word. And along with the refrain came a flash of John and her parked in a pasture off the dirt road that wound away from the back of his house. The night was black, not a star visible through the dusty windshield of his old truck. A warm breeze tiptoed through the rolled-down windows. A horse whinnied from one of the nearby fields. Another one answered.

And there wasn't another person in the world. Just the two of them on that old vinyl bench seat, her head on his shoulder, his arm tucking her into him. The intensity of her feelings for him had been overwhelming. She remembered this clearly, how they had filled her up, and like helium, made her feel as if she could float. Until she met John, Olivia had never known that sense of absolute security. With him, she felt completely safe. It didn't matter that she would be yelled at when she got home. *What were you doing out so late? Giving people something to talk about, I guess. I'm not gonna have any daughter of mine give me reason to be ashamed to show my face in town.*

She'd heard the words so many times that she just knew to expect them. But somehow she had been able to forget their ugliness when she and John were together. With John she had been able to see ahead to the future. To know that things wouldn't always be the way they were. That they would make a life together where no one ever shouted or slammed doors. Or hit their daughters.

She closed her eyes and willed her thoughts in a different direction, swallowing back the hurt that had resurfaced with it.

"You remember this song?"

She looked up at him, feeling off-balance.

"I guess we must have played it until the tape literally wore out."

She was surprised he remembered, yes. Because this wasn't the same John whose visible resentment had flattened her at Dickson's that morning. This was the John of old. She heard it in his voice. Something squeezed at Olivia's heart and filled her with gratitude for his reappearance. She'd thought him gone to her forever. Just a glimpse of him, even temporarily, was an unexpected gift.

"I'd find one song I liked, and that was it. I had to hear it over and over."

"I liked it, too." He looked down at her, his voice low and easy, a softness in his eyes that pulled at something deep within her. Her cheeks were suddenly warm, too warm, and her mind filled with images of the two of them, of the first time they'd made love in the back of John's truck, the ridges of the metal bed pressing into her back through the blankets beneath them, his warm hands on her skin, the stars as their ceiling and this song in the background.

The memory was as intimate as memories get, and the fact that they were remembering it together, here on this dance floor with more than two hundred people around them made it all the more piercing.

John's arm tightened around her waist, the adjustment slight enough to make her wonder if it had been her imagination, if he himself was aware of it. They danced there among classmates who had married years before and were still together, among others who had renewed old friendships, old attractions.

But for Olivia, for the duration of that song, it was just the two of them, dancing alone under the stars.

DID THEY HAVE any idea how right they looked together?

From the vantage point of Cleeve Harper's arms, Racine decided there was something about the two of them that seemed predetermined long ago. John Riley and Olivia Ashford just fit, they complemented one another the way a man and woman should.

The recognition of it hit her with a little stab of envy. It was a shame they couldn't see what the rest of the world saw.

"You're a good dancer."

She glanced up to find Cleeve looking down at her with an odd expression in his eyes. "Thank you," she said. "You're pretty good at railroading a girl onto the dance floor yourself."

"A man does what he must," he said, smiling.

Racine sighed. If she knew what was good for her, she'd let him find another partner after this song ended. But for reasons she'd be the first to admit weren't in her best self-interest, she ignored the voice of common sense, and they danced on a while longer. Cleeve told her silly jokes with corny punch lines in his boisterous voice. And Racine laughed. The kind of laughter that made her stomach hurt. She hadn't done a lot of laughing the last few years. Doing so now with Cleeve felt like taking up exercise after years of being sedentary.

The music slowed down, and Cleeve drew her in a little closer. Attraction swirled inside her, and she wished, just for a moment, that this was real, that they were both free to pursue it.

Cleeve told her about the alfalfa he'd baled that afternoon, the prettiest he'd had in a couple of years. Racine asked questions, basic stuff—how do you know when it's ready to cut? Do you really get up at three-thirty every morning to milk the cows? She'd always loved the idea of living on a farm, of having animals to take care of, fields to walk in.

It was obvious to her that Cleeve loved what he did every day of his life. She recalled a few of the comments she'd overheard Macy Harper make to other people in the post office, of how she lived for the day when she could convince him to sell that stinking place.

"You and Jimmy split for good?"

Racine looked up at Cleeve's for-once serious expression. "Signed the final papers three days ago. That's pretty much for good as far as I'm concerned."

He appeared to consider that, sent his gaze off to the other end of the crowd and then wound it back to her face where it stayed. "You are one stunning woman, you know that, Racine?"

Warmth welled up inside her, followed arms and legs to fingers and toes. If laughter had been scarce in her life, then compliments had become extinct. She'd forgotten how good they could feel coming from a man to whom a woman felt a definite attraction. There was no denying it, she was attracted to Cleeve Harper. He thought she was stunning. And so it took every bit of fortitude she could muster to say, "Thank you, Cleeve. But I make it a rule not to get into this kind of conversation with married men. If you ever find yourself outside of that institution, then give me a call. I sure do like compliments."

THE DJ HAD decided it was time to change the mood with the next song, sending the intensity level of the music back up to a nine or so on a scale of one to ten. John and Olivia parted with awkward politeness. She went one way. He went the other. He found a spot on the sidelines where he made a good effort to get a handle on the feelings storming through him, old tangling up with new until he failed altogether at differentiating between the two.

John's gaze fell across Liv where she stood now, some fifty yards away, talking to Lori, their heads tipped together, smiles on their faces. The ease of their friendship was apparent, even from this distance, their gestures familiar and their laughter frequent. Some well-buried part of him envied that. Or maybe it wasn't so well-buried.

With distance as a shield, he let himself study her now. In his arms just minutes before, he'd barely been able to look at her, afraid that if he did, he would never look away again. And so he'd absorbed her presence like a blind person using his other senses. The smell of her, something fresh and appealing like spring rain. The feel of her, the skin of her hand soft in his. The sound of her breathing, a little too breathless for a woman as fit as she appeared to be.

"Y'all looked awfully good out there."

Cleeve had sidled up beside him, the expression on his face wavering between hope and chagrin. Hope, surely, that John wasn't going to deck him. Chagrin, most certainly, because he knew he was in the doghouse. "So, what exactly do you think I should extract for the price of that little stunt?" John asked.

"My first born?"

"That'd be letting you off easy."

"Aw, come on, John. The signals going off between you two could knock a satellite out of orbit. Am I wrong about that?"

"Dead."

"Disagree, old buddy. I know lust when I see it. Not that I think there's anything logical about it. I mean it would have been a lot simpler if Mother Nature had made physical attraction an analytical thing. Set it up as a point system. Ten merits for niceness. Like does she brake for small animals? Is she kind to children?'' He scratched the stubble on his jaw. ''And maybe ten merits for cooking skills. Does she make great coffee or lousy coffee? Can she make a mean steak and potato, or are you going to be stuck eating peanut butter sandwiches every night for the rest of your life?''

John folded his arms across his chest and gave his friend a long, hard look. ''Does this theory of yours apply to you and Racine?''

Cleeve attempted surprise and failed. ''She's a nice gal who's had a pretty good run of bad luck.''

''Like you said, Mother Nature's not always logical. And I saw the way you were looking at her out there.''

Cleeve sighed. ''Sometimes I wonder why Macy ever married me. I can't remember the last time she actually smiled at me. We're like two strangers living under the same roof. Seems like married people ought to like each other well enough to smile once in a while.''

''I was just wondering when you were going to wake up and smell that particular pot of coffee.''

''Why does all this stuff between men and women have to be so complicated?''

''I sure as heck don't know the answer to that,

Cleeve, but do me a favor, okay? I don't need you playing matchmaker between Liv and me. You're wasting your time.''

"Aw, John, I wasn't going to—"

"How long have I known you?"

"Long enough?"

"Right. So don't bother to deny what you had in mind.''

"One thing I do know," Cleeve said, an uncharacteristic note of seriousness in his voice. "You've had sadness in your eyes and on your face for too long. I didn't see it when you were dancing with Olivia just now.''

John's denial never made it to his lips. Because it was then, standing there beside his oldest friend in the world, that he put definition to what he'd felt out there with Liv a little while ago. Happiness. It had been happiness.

CHAPTER NINE

Detours

OLIVIA INSISTED ON staying to help Lori clean up. It was almost twelve-thirty, and nearly everyone had already left.

Olivia's feet hurt. The strappy sandals she'd worn all night had rubbed a blister on the side of her foot. Lori had one on her heel. They both took off their shoes, and with sighs of relief, walked around barefoot, laughing. Lori shook her head. "Can you imagine fifteen years ago either one of us letting go of our vanity long enough to admit we had blisters?"

"So there's one positive thing about getting old," Olivia said, still smiling.

The cleanup was minimal. The two of them folded tablecloths, filled a couple of trash bags with plastic cups and plates, righted a few chairs that had fallen over, picked up stray cigarette butts. And for the better part of an hour, while they worked, they talked about who had changed the most, the least, how Sally Amos had six children and still managed to have one of the best figures there—where was the fairness in that?—about anything and everything except what Olivia knew Lori had been dying to ask for the past two hours.

"So what was it like?" Lori finally succumbed to her curiosity.

"What's that?" Olivia asked, buying time.

"Dancing with John."

"Believe me, it wasn't his idea. Cleeve didn't give him a choice."

"So that explains the first song. What about the second and the third?"

For that, Olivia didn't have an answer. Because she'd wondered, too.

THEY LEFT Rolling Hills shortly after 1:00 a.m., telling each other to be careful and promising they would talk in the morning.

Olivia wasn't in the least bit sleepy, even though she'd barely slept the night before. She was wide awake, finally able to take apart the evening's events now that she was alone with no one to interpret her silences.

She'd only seen John one other time after they'd danced together, and that had been a mere glimpse of him heading through the yard toward his house just before midnight. Something as inane as a dance between two people who had been all but forced into the act should not have stirred up such a hornet's nest of memories. But it had, and for Olivia it was imperative that she put them to rest because they could only lead her into a nowhere of what-ifs and maybes.

She followed the road back to town at well under the speed limit, unaware of her intention to take the turnoff onto 134 until she'd actually done so. The road led across a double set of railroad tracks and down a narrow stretch of hardtop that ran through what had been farmland when she'd lived here. There were now two subdivisions where there had once grown corn and winter wheat. It hardly looked like the same place.

Within a couple minutes, she left the subdivisions behind, and the road turned to country again, her headlights illuminating fields dotted with big round bales of hay, modest homes whose value wasn't in the size of their structure, but in the space around them. Having lived most of her adult life in cities where buildings were spaced inches apart, Olivia had a new appreciation for this.

Another few minutes, and there it was. The turn lay just ahead. She tapped on the brakes. Her mind said no, but something else pushed her on, some need to see if the old place had changed.

The road wasn't paved. Time had filled it with potholes and made it almost impassable. She steered the car around them as best she could. The tires dropped off every few seconds, spinning and groaning their way back over the edges. Bushes had grown out into the road, swatting the sides of the car as she passed. The road wound on for a quarter mile. And then, the house was there in front of her. She stopped the car and sat there staring at it, her heart pounding.

It wasn't my fault. It wasn't my fault.

The words marched through her head, a silent mantra she had long ago accepted with the objectivity that had come from a therapist walking her through the past, forcing her to look at it, assess what she could have done differently, what she could not have done.

She reached in the glove compartment for a flashlight, then got out, the heavy *ka-thump* of the closing car door too loud in the stillness.

The house looked much the same, and yet different, like a person who has aged beyond fairness. The basic features hadn't changed, but were burdened now with neglect. The paint on the white clapboard had faded and peeled. Vines climbed the sides of the concrete block chimney and the front steps sagged in the middle. The right side of the porch drooped like a sad, resigned smile.

She went around back, wading through knee-high grass. The screen door that led into the kitchen hung limply to one side as if someone had landed it a good left hook. The breeze tipped it back and forth, and it creaked in protest. Olivia lifted the door and placed it on the other hinge. Silence. She thought she might have preferred the noise.

The wooden door behind the screen was unlocked. Surprised, she pushed it open, then tossed the beam of the flashlight across the kitchen floor. All the furniture was still there, covered with dust and spider webs. Fast-food wrappers and an assortment of beer cans littered the floor as if someone passing through had set up camp here for the night.

The old red linoleum-top table and the four chairs whose seats had long since lost any cushioning were still there. The refrigerator had a cinder block propping open the door. The four-burner stove was pulled away from the wall with the electrical cord dangling over the top. The curtains were the same ones Olivia's mother had made, off-white with now-faded strawberries on them. Equally faded came an image of her mother sitting at her sewing machine hemming those curtains, so pleased with how they'd turned out and how cheerful they would make the small kitchen. If they'd only been able to do the same for their home.

The living room was straight ahead. Olivia stopped in the doorway between the two rooms and let the light find the old couch, which for some reason was standing on end, as if someone had planned to move it out and then decided against it. Her mother's piano sat by the window, and Olivia's heart hurt for all the years it had sat here, for the music it had never made.

Just off the living room was her bedroom. The door was closed, and she considered leaving without opening it. But like the rest of the house, she needed now to see it. She turned the knob and pushed it open.

The flashlight beam revealed the twin bed that had been hers in its place beneath the window, the little-girl-pink spread still covering the mattresses. Her dolls sat in the corner against the wall, looking lonely and forlorn. For the most part, things were just as they'd been. She hadn't expected that, but had imagined the place emptied by looters after so many years. She'd regretted many times not coming back for the few things that had good memories attached.

And there were a few. For the most part her father's constant anger at the world had been directed at her mother who had spent her days trying to avoid setting off his temper. When Elizabeth Ashford had died of pneumonia just before Olivia's ninth birthday, Olivia had simply taken her mother's place. She had not known that life could be any other way. It wasn't until she was in the fourth grade that she'd discovered that other people's families were different. She had spent the night at Lori's because her father had to stay overnight at the hospital, and she had become even more determined to hide what went on in her own house. Surely, she had done something to cause it, must be somehow responsible for it, must have done something somewhere along the way to deserve it. Families who loved one another did not live this way.

Another memory surfaced. This one she shied away from, a mere glimpse of it finding old bruises on her heart.

She had loved her father. And for much of her young life had wanted desperately to figure out why he was always so angry. Why he yelled at her mama, cut her down so that she eventually lost all confidence in her ability to do anything as simple as choosing groceries for the week. Once, Olivia had raised her hand in Sunday school and asked her teacher what God did to people who made other people feel bad about themselves.

"Do you mean intentionally, dear?" Mrs. Myers had asked, looking at Olivia over the top of her wire-rimmed glasses.

Olivia had thought about that for a second, then answered as honestly as she could because if a person did the same thing over and over again, then wasn't it intentional? "I think so."

"Well, dear, that would be a sin. And if we don't ask God to forgive us for our sins and then change the things that we do wrong, we will go to hell."

For Olivia, Mrs. Myers's answer had felt like the time in second grade when she'd gotten hit in the

stomach with a football. She'd felt sick for the rest
of the class and all through church. When they'd
gotten home, her mama had put her on the couch
with a glass of ginger ale and a cold cloth to her
forehead, sure she'd picked up a bug of some sort.
Olivia couldn't stop crying. Later that night, her
daddy had sat on the couch and let her put her head
on his lap, his efforts at comfort clumsy but sincere.
It had been a rare moment when her parents' mutual
concern for her allowed peace to fill the house instead of rage. And all Olivia could think of was what
Mrs. Myers had said that morning, and the awful
thought of her daddy ending up in hell and that there
must surely be some way she could prevent that.

But she had not been able to change her father or
his anger. And so, she had become a master at pre-
tending. No one guessed what her life at home was
like. Not her teachers or her classmates. She made
up stories, taking bits and pieces from things she
heard the other children say, changing a few details
here and there, so they sounded like her own. And
she wore long sleeves to hide the bruises on her
arms, even in the springtime. When the teachers
questioned her about it, she simply said she didn't
like to be cold.

She had made it through high school without a
single teacher ever knowing. Not even John had
guessed, teasing her for looking so graceful and being so clumsy.

Had she confided in him, maybe things would have turned out differently. Maybe she had been wrong not to do so. But she had been sure it was a flaw in her that made her father act as he had. Maybe John would see the same thing in her; maybe it would change the way he felt about her. So she'd kept quiet until it was too late for anyone to help her.

After she'd left Summerville, her father had taken a job with a construction company that moved around the country. He had died alone in a hotel room in North Carolina, and Olivia had received a call from the job foreman who had tracked her down through some insurance information in her father's wallet. She'd had him buried in a little cemetery in Mount Jackson, Virginia, where he'd grown up and where his mother and father had been buried. It seemed hypocritical to bury him next to her mother when there had been no peace in their lives together.

Olivia had never once come back here, simply leaving the place as it was, as her father had left it.

She went outside. An owl hooted somewhere in the nearby woods. Olivia sat on the worn concrete steps, the owl's mournful call echoing her almost unbearable sense of loss for all that could have been. For everything that had not been. For the father who had never seen the wrong in the way he had mistreated his family. For the love of a boy she'd thought real and true. And for the child she had never had a chance to know.

IT WAS ALMOST two in the morning, and John had reached that point just beyond bone tired. He'd driven Cleeve home from the reunion after his truck had failed to start, and forty-five minutes worth of tinkering had done nothing but give John more fodder for ribbing him about his choice in vehicles. He was a Dodge man. Cleeve a Ford.

This particular stretch of 134 was as straight as a Kansas road. A half-mile or so ahead, a car pulled out in front of him, taillights flashing. Closer in, he recognized the BMW, and then the car accelerated, the lights quickly becoming pinpoints in the distance.

He slowed down, frowning. That was Olivia's old driveway. What had she been doing out there this late? He rolled by the turnoff at just over twenty miles an hour, his foot off the accelerator.

Strange as it now seemed, in all the time he and Olivia had dated, he had never once been to her house. She'd always made excuses for not taking him there. He'd been curious, but he'd never pressed her about it. He knew her father worked construction jobs, and that they weren't rich. He hadn't cared. It made no difference to him, but he had noticed how uncomfortable she was at his house when he'd first started taking her there. And although he would have been the last person in the world to make comparisons, he had never wanted to put her in the position of doing so.

He'd driven out here once after she'd left, looking for answers. Her father had answered the door and told him in a flat, cold voice to get off his property.

John turned the truck around now and without giving himself time to reconsider, headed down the driveway, tree limbs hanging past his windshield. How had Liv gotten her car down this road without getting stuck? He idled down the drive, questioning the logic of what he was doing, but he went ahead anyway.

The house was small. A lone rocking chair sat on the narrow front porch. What little gravel there was left of the driveway in front of the house had all but disappeared.

John reached for the flashlight under his seat, got out and made his way through the overgrown yard to the front of the house. It was locked, so he went around back and found the side door ajar. He pushed it open and stepped inside. Maybe this was a mistake. Maybe it was wrong. Maybe it was invading something that should be left alone. The arguments hurled themselves at him, and yet he could not turn around.

The house was all but crumbling from neglect, the smell of mildew strong. He guessed no one had lived here after Liv's father had died twelve years ago. Did she still own the place? He wandered down a hallway. A bedroom. And another.

This had obviously been Liv's. He stepped inside. A bulletin board hung on a side wall, one end crooked as if the nail had slipped down in the old drywall. He shone the light on it. A school lunch menu. An acceptance letter from the University of Virginia, where they had planned to go together. A photo of Liv and him at a football game.

He thought about the young child who had lived here. The teenage girl he had loved. A chest sat against the wall. He opened a drawer. It was full of clothes. Dusty but neatly folded. Shorts. T-shirts. One said: Go Summerville High. State Football Champions. Another said: Orange County Cutting Horse Competition. He'd given it to her.

He opened the drawer beneath it. Full. And so was the bottom one. He went to the closet. Opened the door. Except for a few empty hangers, it was also nearly full.

Why wouldn't she have taken her things with her when she'd moved away?

He crossed the room and sat on the bed, trying to make sense of it. Why would Liv have left here and not taken her things with her?

A nightstand sat by the bed. He pulled open the drawer on the front and sent up another cloud of dust. Inside was an assortment of pens, pencils and loose-leaf paper. He started to slide it shut, but it stuck and he gave it a tug. It didn't budge and he yanked again. The drawer gave with a groan, popping out of the stand. The contents toppled to the floor.

He leaned over, upended the drawer and began picking things up. Something on the bottom caught his eye. He pointed his flashlight at it. A packet of letters tied together with a red ribbon. Like the ones Liv used to write him. They were held in place with a piece of wire that had been tacked to the wood. Alarms sounded inside him. *Put it back, John. They're not yours to read.*

Piece by piece, he retrieved everything from the floor and put it all back inside. Including the letters. He closed the drawer. But he sat there, feeling the pull of them. Wondering if they held any answers to what had gone wrong between Liv and him.

As a grown man with an entire life between then and now, he should have been able to let it to go. But there was enough of the hurt boy still left inside him to need to look.

He opened the drawer again and pulled out the bundle. A heart had been drawn on the back of the paper with John and Olivia written inside. He untied the ribbon. Started to tie it back. Then yanked it off. He unfolded the letter on top of the stack and began to read.

John,

You picked me up at the end of the driveway tonight. Don't know how to explain this to you, so I just don't. It's kind of awkward, and I wonder what it would be like to live in a house where I'd be glad to have you pick me up at the front door. Not a big fancy house. Just a house where it's obvious somebody loves it and the other people who live there.

We drove up to Starkey Mountain again tonight. Talked. About what we want to do with our lives. The places we'd like to go. You said Ireland because everything is so green there and that you'd like to take me with you. I can't imagine such a thing, actually leaving here, but I'm seventeen now, and maybe Daddy will be wrong about me dreaming bigger than I am. Maybe I'll do something really incredible with my life, go to all those wonderful places you and I talk about.

Wouldn't that be something?

You make me think it really could happen. I loved it when you spread one of Sophia's old quilts out in the back of the truck tonight, and we lay there on it, studying the sky. You said you were impressed with how many of the constellations I knew. That I'm the smartest girl you've ever known. But that's not true, I don't think. I just remember things I've read.

The letter ended there. He flipped open the next one.

We kissed again tonight. Sweet kisses that make me believe what I see in your eyes when you look at me might actually be love. Which is about the hardest thing I could ever imagine trying to believe. You could have any girl in school. Why would you want me? I don't know, but when you put your arms around me, a feeling knots up in my stomach, almost a pain, it's so strong. Is this love? Is that what it means to want someone so much that you almost wish you'd never met because the fear of losing this feeling wakes you up at night and is the first thing you think of in the morning?

An ache set up in John's chest. He opened the next letter.

I don't know how long what you and I feel for each other will last, if it'll be forever or if it will be gone tomorrow. Maybe it doesn't matter. Maybe it isn't love that you feel. But for now, I'd like to believe that it is. I'd like to believe that someone as deeply good as you could love me.

You asked me about the bruises again tonight. I said I ran into the bathroom door. I wish I didn't have to lie to you.

Stunned, John opened the last of the pack.

So much has happened in these last few weeks.
Or maybe it's just that I've been too afraid to
put the words on this page. Because that makes
them real. I've never been so scared in my life.
I wish I could find the courage to tell you, John.
What am I going to do?

John refolded the last letter, not sure what to
think, too numb to feel anything.

He remembered now how she'd always had a
bruise somewhere. Had her father hit her? Had it
been because of him? Was that why she'd left Summerville? Why she'd been so scared?

He tried to separate the mass of what he felt into
individual pieces, take each of those apart one by
one. Rage. Tenderness. Terror. Longing. Regret. But
suddenly, the walls of the space inside him where
he'd long ago sealed away his feelings for Liv Ashford strained at their beams and frame, pushing upward and outward until all the nails holding them
popped free, and emotion flooded through him.

With the letters still in his hand, he vaulted off
the bed and ran from the house, certain if he stayed
a moment longer, he would drown.

A SHORT WHILE LATER, John opened the door to his
daughter's room, stood just inside, saying a silent

prayer of thanks for the child curled up on the pale green sheets, a Mickey Mouse night-light sending off its yellow glow of reassurance on the wall just below her. Charlie lay at the foot of the bed. She raised her head and gave him a sleepy, questioning look. He motioned for her to stay where she was. The dog put her head back down and closed her eyes.

It was late, and he didn't want to wake Flora, but the need to see his daughter burned inside him, so he crept quietly across the thick rug to the bed. He sat down on the corner beside her, reached out and smoothed her soft hair from her cheek, tucked it behind her ear. She made a snuffling noise and curled up a little tighter under the sheet.

John's gratitude for this child went beyond thankfulness. Her unconditional love for him was one of the greatest gifts life would ever give him. To abuse that love, not respect it for the cherished thing that it was, went beyond anything he could ever imagine.

Anger at Liv's father roared inside him. He let it burn, while he thought of the young Liv he had known and the lengths to which she must have gone to keep what happened in her house a secret. How many times had he questioned a bruise on her arm, her wrist? They came back to him now and he saw them for what they were.

Each one sickened him.

Had anyone else known? Somehow, he knew the

answer was no. She had managed to keep it a secret from everyone. A child who spent her life trying to hide such a secret from the world had no childhood.

He reached out and pulled his sleeping daughter into the curve of his arms, rested his chin on her soft hair, reached for the stuffed monkey that had been on the bed beside her, and stayed there with her until the ink of night dried to day.

CHAPTER TEN

Back Roads

OLIVIA AWOKE the next morning aware that something was different.

Lying there in the early-morning stillness, she felt the change inside herself. It was as if she'd been cut loose somehow. Freed. As if some hard, cold place within her had warmed. And inside it was peace. As if by going back to her old house last night and confronting the ghosts there, she had acknowledged the hold they had once held over her, but at the same time, had seen that they no longer had any power.

She should have done something with the house long ago, but it had been easier just to leave it alone, let the weeds grow up around it and her memories of it as well. Maybe after she got back to D.C., she would call a real estate agent and put the place up for sale.

It was time. Past time.

Maybe, though, it was past time for a lot of things. For so long, she had imposed rules upon herself. Staying single. Keeping her life free of commitment. Of risk. Not considering the possibility of ever being a mother.

She thought of Flora and of Lori's four beautiful children, and something painful echoed inside her. Long ago, she had never imagined living her life without children. And yet here she was. Thirty-three years old and single with no prospects of being anything different.

Had she done this intentionally, too? Was this one more way, conscious or not, she had found to punish herself for not preventing the loss of her child, John's child? Would she spend the rest of her life repeating that same punishment? Or was it time to let the blame she had leveled at herself go?

The question was still with her an hour later when she left her room at the bed-and-breakfast to go for a run. The change this morning was in her physical self, too, in her step, her stride, her whole demeanor. She felt lighter, as if she'd been released from the anchor of memories to which she'd long ago chained herself.

Even at this early hour, the air held enough stickiness to predict the humid summer day ahead. But the sky was already that deep Virginia June blue, not a single cloud in sight.

A little after eight o'clock, the town was up. From the bakery on the corner of Main and Fourth came a tantalizing waft of fresh bread. Old Mr. Carlyle still ran the place. He was outside sweeping the sidewalk, making neat little piles of the scattered leaves and candy wrappers to scoop up with his dustpan. "Morning, Mr. Carlyle," Olivia said, jogging by.

He glanced up, pausing in mid-sweep, his smile wide and genuine. "Morning, young lady. Looks like a beautiful day ahead."

"It sure does," she said.

A block down, Jim Carter was opening up the corner drugstore. A sign in the front window blinked Fresh Squeezed Lemonade. A fluffy, gray cat sat beneath the sign on the stone sill.

If things hadn't changed, the Saturday-morning rush would take place around ten o'clock when everyone came into town for weekly grocery shopping at Singleton's, which sat just ahead on the corner. Olivia and her mother had driven to town every Saturday and bought their groceries there. She had always let Olivia push the cart and pick out a still warm-from-the-oven peanut butter cookie from the bakery counter.

So far, the town had not succumbed to the huge discount and mega stores sprouting up in America's small towns, leaving their centers to dry up and die. She had forgotten, perhaps deliberately, how much she had loved this place. The thought of D.C. on this beautiful summer morning felt like a sweater that had gotten too tight and would never be comfortable again.

Ten minutes into the run, Olivia had broken a good sweat and was glad she'd left her running jacket behind in favor of the sleeveless white tank top. She followed Main Street out of town where it turned into Route 121 and led out into the country.

There was plenty to look at along the way. Dairy farms with their black-and-white cows heading back out to pasture single-file after being milked, an orchard whose trees were loaded with tiny peaches, a beautiful old farm house someone had long ago abandoned that now stood in sad neglect with round bales of hay stacked across the front porch, shutters drooping.

A truck engine rumbled up from behind. She glanced over as it went past. John? His truck had an empty stock trailer hooked to the back. Her heart kicked up. The brake lights flashed, and the rig slowed then stopped altogether in the middle of the road. Olivia kept running, not sure whether she should just wave and go on or stop. Awkwardness gripped her in a vise usually reserved for sixteen-year-olds.

She slowed to a walk just before she reached his window. It was rolled down, and he threw up a hand, accompanied it with a nod. His eyes were hidden behind a pair of black sunglasses, the small square kind that wouldn't have looked any better on Tom Cruise than they did on him. A dark-blue baseball cap with AQHA stitched across the front sat low on his forehead. "You're out awfully early this morning," he said, his voice still uneven at the edges, as if he'd just gotten up or had endured a night as short on sleep as hers had been.

"I could say the same for you," she said.

"I called Lori to see where you were staying. Mrs. Stanley at the bed-and-breakfast said you'd headed down Main Street to go for a run. Thought I'd see if I could track you down."

A response completely eluded her. He'd deliberately come looking for her this morning? Why? "Is everything all right?" she asked.

He held her gaze for a long moment while two crows on the fence by the road started up a shouting match. "I just wondered if you might like to ride with me out to Cleeve's. I was headed over there to pick up some calves."

Olivia wasn't sure what she had expected him to say, but that would have been close to the last thing.

"Probably not the most exciting offer you've had this weekend," he said, when she failed to respond. He smiled, not a full-fledged smile, but a halfway, uncertain one, as if he really wanted her to say yes, but thought she probably wouldn't.

That arrow went straight to Olivia's heart. To hide her own fluster, she reached down and retied a running shoe that didn't need retying. Why not? One weekend out of the rest of her life. Not to go would be to give herself a case of permanent regret. She stood and nodded. "I'd love to come along."

His smile deepened, and she caught a glimpse of the old John. Color rushed to her face and stole whatever response had been making its way to her lips. "I better get this thing out of the middle of the road though, before somebody runs over us," he said.

"Okay." She jogged around the back of the trailer, fifteen emotions jostling for prominence all at once. John reached across the seat and opened the door, his gaze meeting and holding hers, the moment brief but meaningful in some way she could not explain.

He shifted gears, and the truck moved out with a low roar.

And all she could think was *I must be dreaming this.* She turned her gaze to the summer green of the trees, the grass that had grown nearly waist high on the shoulders of the road. They passed a field where two horses, one black, one gray, stood head to tail alongside the fence, swatting flies for one another. In the next pasture up, a group of butter-colored cows loitered beside a big blue metal container, licking molasses from a conveyor belt. The scenes were familiar. They filled her with the kind of homesickness that felt bone-deep and made her dread the thought of going back to the city.

"So what's it like, living in D.C.?" John's question echoed her thoughts.

"Trying at times. I miss all this." She looked out the window again. "I've never let myself think too much about the differences. Maybe that's a good thing."

"I remember one time when I was about seven or eight telling my dad that when I grew up I was going to move somewhere flat. That I was sick of all the hills and mountains around here. That flat was prettier. And he said he guessed that could be so, but someday I was going to realize that it didn't really matter whether the land around me was flat or hilly, what mattered was whether it felt like home or not."

"I think I'd have to agree with that," she said. "Lori told me your father passed away a few years ago. I was really sorry to hear it."

"He was a good man. He lived a good life. Tried to set the right example for me. I don't know that we can ask for more than that." He looked at her then, his eyes hidden behind the dark glasses. "Liv. I owe you an apology for being such a jackass the last couple of days."

Her name on his lips, that old nickname only he had ever called her, raised goose bumps on her arms. She looked down at her lap. The truck rolled over a pothole in the road, and the stock trailer behind rattled in complaint. "John, you don't have to—"

"No, I do."

"Apology accepted," she said.

They drove on for a little while, something shifting between them, the silence comfortable in a way that stirred up old feelings inside Olivia, beckoned a yearning for the way things had once been between them. She remembered how they'd be riding along in his first truck, and he would reach across and take her hand, his thumb thumping out the beat to some song on the radio.

He looked at her again, glanced down at her hand resting on the arm of her seat, and she knew, just knew somehow, that he was remembering the same thing.

She jerked her gaze back to the road and sought neutral conversation. "Is Cleeve still running his family's dairy?" she asked too quickly.

John nodded. "Yep. He takes a lot of pride in that farm."

"Is he married?"

"He is. Not all that happily, but married."

"I'm sorry to hear that."

"He's a good man. He just hasn't found the right woman."

"I'm glad you two have stayed friends." It would have been hard to explain why if he had asked, because it had something to do with her knowing that Cleeve thought of John as a brother, and he'd always made it a priority to watch out for him. To Olivia, there was something comforting about that.

"Have you had breakfast?"

She shook her head. "No."

"There's a little place up ahead where I stop sometimes when I'm out this way. Nothing fancy. But the coffee's respectable, the food's good."

"I didn't bring any money with me."

"How about I pay and you can load the trailer out at Cleeve's?"

She raised an eyebrow. "I may regret this."

The sign came up on the left within a half-mile or so. Pearl's. Fill Up With Good Food And Gas Before You Leave.

"The wording has been questioned more than once." John smiled. "Pearl's canned answer is 'I'm not wasting good money on another sign when everybody knows what I meant.' I think she actually printed it up and taped it to the cash register."

Olivia pressed her lips together to keep from laughing. She was still smiling when he hit his blinker and slowed down, easing the truck and trailer into the gravel parking lot where there were enough cars to prove the sign hadn't hurt business. John pulled into a space at the edge of the lot and cut the engine. It was amazing to be riding down this country road with him on a beautiful summer morning, laughing about Pearl's sign. Amazing and yet right. Scary how right it felt.

"Nice morning. Any interest in eating outside?" John asked once they were out of the truck.

"Sounds great. I'll get us a table if you'll order for me."

"Deal. You want to go in and take a look at the menu first?"

"No need. Just pick me out something with real fat in it," she said.

He smiled. "You're definitely at the right place."

Olivia headed for the picnic tables in the grass to the side of the store, her stomach doing a muffled rumble at the aroma of bacon and eggs wafting out the front door. John had stopped just short of the entrance to talk to someone. His back was to her, and her gaze caught and hung on the sturdy width of his shoulders, the curve and indention of the muscles in the arms folded across his chest as he laughed at something the man next to him had just said.

Olivia had no idea what she was doing here. Or what had caused the change between them this morning. Normally, she would have taken the situation apart, dissected it for bits of evidence to support whichever argument seemed most likely. But this morning, she just wanted to be here. And to enjoy it while it lasted. That was enough.

John turned just then and caught her gaze, as if he'd known she was looking at him. For the life of her, she could not look away. Some well-submerged feminine instinct rallied and wanted him to know she'd been looking, that she still found him over-whelmingly attractive.

It was a moment cut away from the others sur-rounding it. He had taken his sunglasses off, holding them in his right hand. She was glad, because she recalled then how it was never the color of his eyes she remembered when she thought of them. It was this, the look in them when he saw her, in that initial moment before he had time to censor his response: untethered gladness, appreciation, attraction. She re-membered this because no one had ever looked at her with that combination of intensity, before or since. Until now.

The moment couldn't have lasted more than three or four seconds. And yet everything inside her shifted and moved. Like platelets in the earth whose movement permanently alters the landscape above.

Shaken, she dropped her gaze and headed for a table.

Ten minutes later, John came back out with their food in a brown paper bag. "Sorry," he said. "They're a little busy this morning."

"It was nice just sitting out here," she said, her former bravado now gone altogether. She kept her gaze focused just short of his, chattering on about how good the food smelled, how warm the sun al-ready was, and then she stopped, hearing herself.

Olivia had never been one to chatter.

John wasn't saying anything. He was just looking

at her with an intensity that melted something deep inside her. "Hope you like this," he said, glancing down then and pulling out of the bag some bundles wrapped in white paper.

"If it tastes as good as it smells—"

John handed Olivia one bundle, along with a plastic cup of orange juice.

"Thank you," she said, and opened it to reveal a four-inch-high bacon-and-egg biscuit. "That's a ten-miler if I ever saw one."

John smiled. "You said lots of fat."

Olivia took a bite and decided then and there that it would be worth every extra mile she had to run to make up for it. John had gotten the same thing, and they ate in companionable, appreciative silence while Olivia thought how nice it was to hear his laughter again, how much she had missed it, how gratifying it was to be the one to prompt it.

"I can't remember when I enjoyed anything more than that," she said, when she'd finished the last bite. "I guess the feminine thing to do would have been to offer you the last half of mine. But that was just too unbelievable."

"I'll tell Pearl you said so next time I see her."

They sat there on the wooden seats of the old picnic table, their gazes on one another's face. Searching. Assessing. And the look held for just a second too long in the way of a moment between two people that says This means something. Their smiles tapered off, and the questions hanging between them were all but audible. *What happened to us? It was like this, wasn't it? As good as we're remembering.*

John cleared his throat.

Olivia blinked and sat up straighter.

Then they got busy wadding up their biscuit wrappers, cleaning off the table, dropping the remnants of their breakfast in the nearby trash can while feelings she had thought time would have dulled into non-existence swooped through her. Wrong! They existed. Oh, they existed.

On the walk back across the parking lot, she couldn't look at him, but knew his gaze was on her. She savored the pleasure in that, however short-lived it might be.

The silence between them strung out while they got back in the truck, hooked up seatbelts, closed doors. They were a mile down the road when John finally said, "So how did you decide to go into broadcasting? I never realized you were interested in it."

"I wasn't. I was doing an internship at a small station. The regular weather girl got sick one day right before going on air, and in a moment of desperation, they shoved me in front of the camera. I was so scared I thought I was literally going to have a heart attack."

John smiled. "I bet there are a few tabloid shows that would love to have a clip of that."

"Scary thought," Olivia said, grimacing.

"It's not something I'd have imagined you doing."

"Me, either," she admitted. "Sometimes I feel like it's not really me doing it."

"What do you mean?"

"Oh, I don't know. Like I'm someone else in front of the camera. Just putting on the mask."

"You make it sound easy. Like anyone could do it. I know that can't be true."

She lifted a shoulder. "I got better over the years. But it's definitely one of those jobs where someone is always revving to take your place."

"So what happened to your dream of being a writer?"

The question sent surprise skidding through her. He had remembered. He was the only person in her life she'd ever voiced that dream to. With the question came an echo of her father's voice. *No point in letting your dreams get bigger than you are, girl. Just means you'll end up bitter and disappointed.* She wondered now, from the perspective of an adult, if that was what had happened to her father. If he'd just never gone after his own dreams for fear of failure, and had spent the rest of his life in bitterness.

To John, she simply said, "I feel lucky to have been given the opportunities I've been given. It seems ungrateful to be disappointed about not doing something I probably wouldn't have been any good at, anyway.''

"I think you would have been damn good," he said. "I've always thought the best writers are the ones who open their hearts and show the world what's inside. That was something I always knew you could do.''

His words warmed her, filled her with the kind of concentrated happiness a person knows can never last, so pure is its intensity. A mile or two more of Lanford County countryside rolled by, and all Olivia could think was how surreal this entire morning had been. As if someone had picked the two of them up out of their lives and set them down in a scene where their past did not exist, their future did not matter.

Maybe it didn't.

Was such a thing possible?

CHAPTER ELEVEN

Circles

IF SOMEONE had told John three days ago that he would be riding down Route 121 East with Liv Ashford in the seat beside him, he would have said it was about as likely as him waking up that morning with wings and flying himself off to Mars.

So he would have been wrong.

And here he was trying to reconcile the importance of what he had learned last night with the fact that he had no idea how to talk to her about it. After all, he had gone inside her old house, uninvited, snooped around and read those letters, which he didn't regret because of what they had brought to light. But he did feel guilty for the act itself.

Should he talk to her about it? Was it actually any of his business now? Would she welcome what she might very well consider meddling on his part?

No ready answer came to him. Doubt kept him silent for now.

They had no sooner pulled into the gravel driveway outside Cleeve's enormous dairy barn than Cleeve himself was striding out the big center door with a grin on his face just about half the size of the opening. "Didn't tell me you were bringing company."

"Kind of last-minute," John said.

"Hey, Cleeve," Liv said, sliding out of the truck.

"Hey, dancing queen," he teased.

"Hah," she said. "Only because you dragged me out there!"

"Looked like she was havin' fun, didn't it, John?"

"That's your kettle of fish, ole' boy, lassoing women onto the dance floor," John said and then added, "Ernie picked your truck up first thing. Said to tell you he'd call you after he got it in the shop and figured out what was wrong with it. You gonna buy a Dodge next time?"

"Right after Ford goes out of business."

Liv smiled. "I see you two haven't settled that argument yet."

John shook his head and found himself smiling back. "Not yet. Aren't you going to offer Liv the grand tour, Cleeve?"

"Sure thing." He hooked an arm through Liv's and led her off toward the barn, motioning for John to follow.

"I remember when we came here on that field trip in tenth grade," Liv said. "You had baby everything. Calves. Rabbits. Chicks. And we got to drink milk fresh from the cow. Was that barn here before?'' she asked, pointing at the one to their right.

''My dad and I just built it a couple years ago,'' Cleeve said, and John knew he was pleased she had noticed. As far as Cleeve was concerned, anybody who showed an appreciation for farm life went directly to the head of the class. John watched Cleeve work his charm with Liv, guiding her from one thing to another—showing her the new milking system they'd been using for the past year, which had increased their production by twenty percent, proud of what he did here in a way that John both understood and appreciated. And while Cleeve talked, he tried to make sense of the events that had taken place this morning, get a rein on the feelings that seemed to be taking on a force of their own inside him.

In the past twelve hours, everything he'd believed to be true had been turned upside down. No more than half a day ago, he'd been able to look at Liv with a semi-neutral eye, keeping himself afloat on the rock-solid raft of anger he'd built as a life-saving device so many years ago.

And maybe there was a certain comfort in that. That anger at Liv made it easy to bury anything else he might have ever felt for her. All those feelings had been submerged beneath the silt of his resentment. He'd never imagined they would ever surface again.

But he had been wrong. Because, like the arrowheads Flora loved to look for in the pastures on their farm, they had made their way back up through the dirt, so that if you knew what you were looking for, they were recognizable.

And he recognized these feelings—he felt a not small stab of terror for their renewal. Because who was he kidding? If it had been possible to die of heartbreak, he would have done so fifteen years ago. He could admit that much now, at least to himself.

How was it that life could send you rolling along on the same straight path just long enough that you got complacent and thought you knew where you were going to end up? For him, that destination had been spending the rest of his life alone. A week ago, he could not have conceived of wanting again, needing again. It was as if he'd gone numb after Laura died, his guilt over the things he should have done, hadn't done, leaving a blank hole inside him.

And then Liv came back. And he'd read those letters last night and understood that he had not known everything there was to know about her and why she'd left this town. All the supports on which he'd rested his anger had fallen out from beneath him, and he was left with feelings of an altogether different kind—the renewal of old emotion and attraction for what remained of the girl he had known.

And the ignition of something new for the woman she was now.

Liv's laughter brought him back to the moment. And the sound of it caused John's heart to knot up.

As had happened all those years before, he felt the shift inside him, the beginning of feelings that were not within his control. He wanted to stop them and knew a wave of panic at his inability to do so. At the sure and certain knowledge that just because they had a past did not mean they could have a future. And surely, a person could not survive that kind of loss twice in one lifetime.

AFTER CLEEVE HAD FINISHED giving Olivia a tour of the farm, he directed them to the front yard of the white farmhouse. They sat under an old maple tree, and he served them iced tea he swore he'd made himself. It was good, and they gave him credit. For Olivia, it was wonderful to listen to John and Cleeve banter back and forth just as they always had, two men who were more brothers than friends.

And being there with them brought back a lot of good memories. Mr. Hawkins, their physics teacher, who wore a white shirt and khaki pants every day, the belt cinched somewhere just below his chest so that the hem of his trousers barely met the tops of his socks. The spring day the three of them had talked Lori into playing hooky and had spent it on the dock at John's pond and how Mr. Richmond, the high-school principal, had driven out there and found them and had made them clean blackboards after school for a week.

And they remembered how Cleeve ate three strawberry popsicles and two ice cream sandwiches every day for lunch, no matter how many times his mother threatened not to give him lunch money if he didn't start ordering the hot plate.

Cleeve shook his head now and pinched his waist-line. "Can you imagine me eating five ice creams a day and being able to get away with it? My one-time furnace metabolism is now a campfire."

"Welcome to your mid-thirties," John said.

"I'm not mid yet," Cleeve protested.

Olivia laughed. And they talked for a while longer about the stuff that wasn't uncomfortable, that didn't get too close to the time when she'd left. They stepped around the subject like a wall in the middle of the road that was easier to skirt by than to try to climb over.

Finally, John looked at his watch and said, "Better get those calves loaded so we can head back."

Olivia couldn't believe how quickly the hours had slipped by, sitting there in Cleeve's yard talking about old times with two people who had been such an integral part of her life that she once couldn't have imagined them not being there. They would always have the bond of beginnings in common. Her friends here in Summerville were different than any of the others she'd made in various places over the years. Lori and Cleeve were her first friends. John, her first love. And being here this weekend had made her see that there was something about those relationships that could never quite be duplicated. They'd been formed in a time of such openness, innocence, a space in life when the heart was so willing and able to let others in, when it hadn't yet been bruised by rejection or any of the other hard knocks waiting ahead in the curves of life's road.

Whatever the reason, she realized the value of them. And she didn't want to let them slip away again.

CLEEVE STOOD in the driveway and threw up a hand as John pulled the loaded trailer out onto the state road in front of the farm.

If that didn't beat all. Seeing those two pull up together this morning was just about the last thing he'd have expected. Nice, though. And when was the last time he'd seen a look like that in John's eyes? Way too long.

Cleeve had loved Laura. She'd been a good woman who had adored John. But Cleeve knew, as only a man's best friend can know, that a part of John's heart had remained permanently closed to her. It wasn't her fault. When Olivia had left here that summer, a part of John had left with her.

Maybe a person could only feel that kind of love once in his life.

Cleeve sent a wishful glance at the house where it seemed as though he spent more and more of his nights alone. It didn't feel like a home to him anymore. He'd grown up there and had thought of it as the place where he wanted to spend the rest of his life. When his mom and dad had given it to him a few years ago, buying themselves a house in town where they could have a little more social life and enjoy their retirement, Cleeve had welcomed the gift.

What had ever made him think Macy could feel the same about this old place? To her, it was more like a prison, a place to escape from. Which she did with more and more frequency.

What was wrong with him that he couldn't find a woman who thought he was okay as he was? He'd be the first to admit there wasn't anything extraordinary about him, but he was beginning to wonder if he was missing something about himself. Three marriages now, two that hadn't worked, and another that was fast on its way to burning out.

He had sworn this was the last time. If this one didn't make it, he was switching to confirmed bachelorhood. But he didn't like being alone. And he wanted children—so badly sometimes it was like a pain inside him that stayed on constant simmer.

I sure do like compliments.

Racine's voice. Lord, she was pretty. And there was no doubt in his mind he was attracted to her. Dancing with her last night had been the most fun he'd had in way longer than he could remember.

But falling for another woman wasn't going to fix anything. He would be jumping from one fire into another. Relationships never started out bad. It was just the opposite. Things were so good on the front end that down the road seemed too far to even bother looking.

Well, his third marriage wasn't over yet. He'd like to think he had it in him to give it his best shot. When Macy got home from seeing her sister Sunday, they would sit down and figure out how to make things work better. Surely, two responsible adults ought to be able to do that.

THEY DROVE the first ten minutes in complete silence. Not uncomfortable, but heavy, as if they both had a lot of questions which they were trying to wrestle into answers.

For Olivia, one continued to persist until she could no longer stand not knowing. "Why did you ask me to go with you today, John?"

He didn't answer right away. And she could tell just by the way the silence grew even heavier that there was a reason. "There's something I need to say to you, Liv," he said finally.

She went still; her heart fluttered and missed a beat. "What is it?"

He flipped the signal and pulled the truck off the road. He took off his sunglasses. "I'm going to ask your forgiveness for this before I even say what I'm about to say. Because what I did was wrong." His voice was serious, his eyes at once apologetic and intent.

She didn't say anything; she couldn't seem to find her voice.

"I went out to your house last night. On my way back from taking Cleeve home, I saw you pulling out of the driveway. I drove in there on some crazy notion that maybe I could figure out what happened to us, Liv. And I found some old letters you'd written to me."

Olivia sat back in the seat, all the air gone from her lungs in a single whoosh. She blinked hard. Then she remembered the letters she'd hidden long ago. Letters she'd written to John knowing she could never actually give them to him. "You...read them?"

"I shouldn't have. I know that. I've tried to find the words to say this all day, but...why didn't you tell me, Liv?"

Olivia had no idea what to think, what to feel, what to say. Everything inside her had gone still, numb, as if a step in any direction might set off an arsenal of mines.

"It doesn't matter now, Liv." He turned in the seat, reached out and pressed the palm of his hand to her cheek. "It's long over. I just wanted you to know that I'm sorry I wasn't there for you. I should have figured it out. All those times you had bruises. How could I have missed it?"

"Don't, John," Olivia whispered, even as she remembered dates with him when she'd been terrified he would notice. Tears welled in her eyes and slipped down her cheeks, as unwelcome now as they were inevitable. And the old shame was there, too, like a second skin that would always be a part of her. "I didn't want you to know."

"Why not?"

"I was embarrassed. Ashamed. Sure there must be something wrong with me."

"Liv." Her name held a thousand layers of emotion, and she knew he would have given anything to change what had been.

He reached out, popped up her armrest and pulled her to him, across the seat and into his arms. Her cheek found his chest, and she could hear his heart beating hard and fast, almost angry-sounding. Her tears left a wet spot on his shirt, and she felt safe and protected as she had not felt once in all the years since they had parted.

The diesel engine of the truck rumbled in neutral. The calves moved around in the trailer behind them, restless. The sun, high in the sky, shone through the windshield and centered its warmth on the two of them, locked in an embrace that conveyed things words simply could not. Comfort, sorrow, regret.

And as far from the reality of their lives as this day was, Olivia chose not to pull away, not to deny that here was a place, a man, whose very familiarity, even with the passage of so many years, made her heart ache with remembrance. They'd been boy and girl the last time they'd held each other this way. But even then, with youthful hormones to cloud all reason, Olivia had sensed the rightness of her place in his arms, had known it would feel the same down the road when they were man and woman. That she would always belong here.

She had been right.

John pulled back and then rubbed his thumb across her tear-stained cheek.

"Come back to the house with me. I can unload these calves, and maybe we'll be in time for lunch. I don't want to let you go yet."

"John, I'm not sure this is a good idea—"

"Liv. Just today. I'm not asking for more than just this day."

And to that, how could she say anything other than yes?

AT THE FARM, John pulled the truck in front of a fenced-in lot, then backed the tail end of the trailer up to the gate. Flora ran across the yard to greet them, pigtails streaming behind her, the golden retriever right at her heels.

"Daddy!"

John got out of the truck and scooped the little girl up in his arms. "Hey, sweet pea. What have you been up to?"

"Hank let me ride Peaches this morning."

"He did?"

She nodded. "And we loped around the ring three times."

John's eyes widened. "Three times?"

"Uh-huh."

"I'm impressed. Flora, you remember Miss Ashford?"

Olivia had gotten out and was standing just to the side of father and daughter.

Flora nodded. "Hi," she said, a little shyly.

"Hi, Flora," Olivia said.

"Why don't you two take Charlie for a swim at the pond while I find Hank and get these calves unloaded?"

"Okay! Come on, Olivia." Flora reached for her hand.

"That's Miss Ashford, unless she's said otherwise," John chided.

"I'd like it if you called me Olivia, Flora."

"I'll be about twenty minutes?" John's gaze met hers.

"Take your time," Olivia said, feeling the

changes between them. She wasn't sure how to act, what to say. With warm cheeks and a slightly off-beat heart, she took the hand Flora offered her, and they set off for the pond.

Charlie led the procession, tail wagging.

"Are you and my daddy dating?" Flora asked when they were halfway between the last barn and the pond.

It was not a question Olivia had expected. Several seconds passed before a reply made it to her lips. "Umm, no. We aren't, Flora."

"Are you friends?"

Even that, Olivia had no idea how to answer. She wanted to be honest with Flora, and yet, she could already see the can of trouble ahead of her just waiting to be opened. "I hope we are."

Flora gave her a long, assessing look that Olivia considered entirely too all-seeing for someone her age. But the answer seemed to satisfy the child, and she sent their conversation off in another direction, now telling Olivia about the treehouse her daddy was building her in their backyard. It was clear what kind of father John was through the way his young daughter spoke of him—with a kind of awe and reverence that left no doubt to anyone listening how much she adored him. Olivia was glad that John had turned out to be exactly the kind of father she had once imagined he would be.

When they reached the dock on the pond, Flora

opened the lid on a wooden storage box where life jackets and a float or two were stored. She dug around for a moment before pulling out a purple Frisbee and calling, "Here, Charlie. Come on!"

Charlie spotted the Frisbee and bolted toward them as if she'd been launched out of a rocket. Flora ran to the end of the dock, her boots thwacking against the wood flooring. She sent the Frisbee flying. Charlie sailed off after it, making a gigantic splash in the still water and then, like an otter, swimming after it.

Charlie returned with the Frisbee in her mouth and climbed up the wooden steps. Once she'd handed it over, she shook and sent water flying. "Charrrlie!" Flora laughed.

For the next fifteen minutes, Olivia and Flora took turns tossing the Frisbee until they ended up as wet as Charlie. And Olivia thought what a beautiful child Flora was, features still round with only a hint of the angles to come. She would be lovely, this Olivia could see. There was her father in her face, dark eyes, smooth skin with its high color in the cheeks. And the reflection of her mother as well, in the straight, even brows, the full pretty mouth.

But there was something more to her appeal. If Olivia had ever had a child of her own, she would have wanted her to be just like Flora. And there on the dock with the sounds of splashing and laughter ringing out against the heat of a June afternoon, she was struck by a feeling of pure happiness for a perfect day, but also by a keen sense of longing for what might have been.

THEY WERE HEADED back across the field with a dripping, exhausted dog when John appeared from behind the barn and called out, "Sophia said if we didn't bring you up to the house for a sandwich, she'd take the apple pie she baked this morning to the church supper tonight instead of serving it for lunch. I've known her long enough to know she means it."

Olivia smiled. "Guess I'll have to take pity on you then."

Flora ran to meet him. "Daddy, we threw the Frisbee for Charlie!"

"You sure you two weren't the ones going in after it?" John laughed, swinging Flora high off the ground.

Watching them, Olivia's heart did a little twist. The same gnawing ache she had felt at Lori's house yesterday nudged her.

John looked at her now. "I see she kept you entertained."

"We had a great time," Olivia said.

They walked to the house, Flora now between them, Charlie lagging behind.

At the back door, John called out, "All right, where's that pie, Sophia?"

"Warming in the oven," she said, meeting them at the kitchen entrance, her kind face beaming. "Well, he did mind his manners and bring you up, after all, Olivia."

"Hi, Sophia. It's wonderful to see you." And it was. Sophia was a barely older version of the woman Olivia had known. Her welcoming smile had not changed one bit.

"Wonderful to see you, child," she said, touching a hand to Olivia's arm. "Come on in here. We're just so pleased to have you."

Sophia led the way to the kitchen. This part of the house had changed very little. The walls were a different color, a soft, warm green and there was a thick wool rug of golds and taupes beneath the harvest-style kitchen table which Olivia did not remember. Laura's touches, she was sure. And she felt a new wave of compassion for the woman who had spent years making this house a home.

"Now, Flora, go wash up," Sophia said. "And in fact, why don't you take Olivia with you? I bet she'd like to get cleaned up since I understand John's had her hauling cows around all morning."

John shook his head as if to say, "What are we going to do with her?"

Flora giggled and reached for Olivia's hand. "Come on, Olivia. I'll show you."

They washed their hands in the half bath down the hall. Olivia listened while Flora told her about

Bible School, which was due to start on Monday night, and how they got to make stuff out of Play-Doh, and how on the last night of the week, the teachers took everybody to Dairy Queen for ice-cream cones. She liked hers dipped in chocolate and extra tall. And while Olivia absorbed this delightful child, the daughter of the man she had once loved, she listened on another level to the sound of John's voice from the kitchen, low and rumbling. The words, she could not distinguish; they didn't matter, anyway. It was the sound that gave her pleasure. And the knowledge that he was so close.

On the way out of the bathroom, Olivia glanced at the living room to her left and thought of how many times she and John had sat in front of the fireplace doing schoolwork, how he'd brought her here on Friday nights to watch a movie on TV and eat popcorn with too much butter.

Now, a picture on the wall to the right of the fireplace caught her attention. A portrait in a gold frame. Olivia stopped, unable to help herself. She recognized the woman at once, her pretty features so like Flora's.

"That's my mommy," Flora said, following Olivia's gaze across the room.

"She was very beautiful," Olivia said. "You look so much like her."

"Do you think so?" Flora asked, and Olivia heard the wistful note in her voice.

"Yes, I most certainly do."

"Daddy says a part of her will always live on through me."

"He's right. And that makes you very special."

"Come on, girls," Sophia called out from the kitchen. "Lunch is ready."

Olivia put her arm around Flora's shoulders, and they trailed back down the hall and into the kitchen. While they were gone, Hank had appeared and was already seated at the round table by the window. When he saw them, he got up, crossed the room and gave Olivia a warm hug. "It sure is good to see you," he said, his voice still sandpaper-rough, and like Sophia's, making her feel welcome.

"You, too, Hank. Time must stand still around here. You and Sophia have hardly changed."

"I'd agree with you as far as Sophia is concerned—she's as pretty as ever, but I'd have to argue with you about myself. Starting to look like a retread."

"You might have a few miles on you, Hank," Sophia threw in from across the kitchen, "but hardly that."

And Olivia would have sworn there was a hint of color in the woman's cheeks.

"Now, y'all sit down and let's eat." Sophia hid her fluster among a bustle of double-checks for the salt and pepper shakers, vinegar for the cucumbers, ice for the water glasses.

The table was set with a huge platter of sandwiches in the middle and an assortment of bowls
scattered around it filled with sliced cucumbers, to-
matoes and green beans from the garden.

Charlie had found a spot in the corner of the
kitchen and was curled up fast asleep, apparently
worn out. Olivia thought how good it felt to be here,
how right, and wondered how that could be when
just yesterday, she had never imagined that she and
John could ever reach a point where this might be
possible.

Sophia and Hank both wanted to know about her
work, thought it awfully exciting and said how
proud they were of her. They were good, warm people. And this was now, as it had once before been,
a place where Olivia felt wanted and welcome.

Of everyone at the table, John was the quietest,
directing only a sentence or two at Olivia throughout
the meal, more out of politeness, she thought, than
anything else. But there were things being said between the two of them that needed no words. Vi-
brations of feeling that did not pretend to have any
basis in reason. They had begun last night when
Cleeve had thrown them together on the dance floor,
had picked up intensity throughout this morning, demanded recognition when he'd held her in the circle
of his arms just a short while ago.

They topped the wonderful meal with Sophia's
apple pie, which in and of itself, was memorable,

strips of crust crisscrossing the top of the glass dish, the center still bubbling hot. Sophia circled the table, topping each of their plates with a scoop of vanilla ice cream.

The men were profuse with their compliments, and Olivia could see that Sophia's role in this family was vital and valued. "Best lunch we've had in ages," from John. "Sophia, you've outdone yourself again," from Hank.

And the chastising, "How am I supposed to believe you two when that's what you always say?" from Sophia was issued with amused appreciation.

Olivia thought how different her own daily life was from Sophia's, with deadlines, expectations, pressures. And although it had its rewards, she did not believe for one moment that her life provided half the satisfaction Sophia's provided to her.

After they'd finished eating, Olivia insisted on helping Sophia with the dishes. Olivia dried while John and Flora put them away.

Once they were done, Sophia said to John, "I promised Flora a trip to Caswell's Five & Dime this afternoon."

"Yaaayy!" Flora said. And then explained to Olivia: "There really isn't hardly anything in there you can buy for a nickel or a dime, but Mr. and Mrs. Caswell don't want to change the name."

"If it were my store, I wouldn't change it, either," Olivia said.

John looked at her and smiled. "Since these two are headed off to town, any interest in going for a ride?"

"If you don't mind that it's been over a decade since I was on a horse."

John's gaze was steady on Olivia's. "I won't let you fall off," he said.

CHAPTER TWELVE

Bittersweet

THEY HEADED for the barn. At one of the pasture gates near the house, John whistled, and five horses at the other end of the field came running. They came to an amazing dead stop right in front of them.

John reached in his pocket, pulled out a handful of sugar cubes and gave them each one. "Caught," he said.

"Just don't ever try to act like you're not a softie," Olivia said, smiling.

He pointed at a galvanized can with a lid on it just to the right of the gate. "Grab a couple halters out of there, and we'll take two of these girls."

Olivia pulled off the lid and handed him two halters with lead ropes attached.

"This is River," John said, as he haltered a pretty little gray mare with big, kind eyes. "And Ellie." He tipped his head at the bay, who was obviously the boss, judging from her irritation at the other horse for getting too close.

John handed River's lead to Olivia, and they led
the two horses down to the barn where they got them
saddled up and spritzed with fly spray. John went
into the tack room and came back out with a pair
of leather chaps. "You're welcome to wear these
over your shorts, if you want. Otherwise that saddle
might have a little bite to it."

Olivia remembered enough about riding to know
he was right. Bare skin against saddle leather
equaled major discomfort. "Thanks," she said, taking the chaps from him and zipping them on.

They led the two mares outside the barn. John
held River's reins until Olivia was in the saddle, a
not exactly graceful undertaking. "You'll pretend
you didn't see that, right?"

John smiled. "Yes, ma'am."

They walked from the barn, John's mare slightly
leading.

A stray cloud weakened the early afternoon sun.
Everything around them was green and teeming with
life. Considering how long it had been since she'd
last ridden, Olivia felt amazingly comfortable in the
big Western saddle, the leather reins soft and well
oiled in her right hand. The mare had a nice, rhyth-
mic walk, her ears perked forward in calm interest
at their surroundings. Olivia relaxed and set her gaze
on the wide shoulders of the man in front of her.
She marveled that the two of them were here in this

space of time, going out for a ride together the way they had so many times when they'd been kids.

With the barn out of sight, they turned onto an old dirt road that wound through a patch of woods. The trees, enormous old oaks and maples, threw criss-crossed shadows across the lane, providing them with instant shade.

"You all right back there?" John called over his shoulder, slowing his mare to let Olivia and River catch up.

"Perfect," she said.

They walked side by side for a minute or two before John said, "Remember this path?"

"It leads to the orchard, right?"

He nodded, looking pleased that she had not forgotten.

But then forgetting such a place would have been impossible. Her stomach knotted at the thought of seeing it again, at allowing back into existence some memories that had no equal.

They rode on for a bit. "Flora is a special little girl, John," Olivia said after a length of silence.

"I'd be the first to admit my prejudice." He kept his gaze on the dirt road before them. His expression changed, the lightness gone. "But that's how a father should feel about his daughter, and if he doesn't, then he doesn't deserve the privilege of having her."

The words were heartfelt. Olivia saw it in the set

of his strong jaw. Flora was a lucky child to have a father who loved her as this man did. And for the first time in her life, Olivia felt pity for her own father and all that he had missed by letting his anger at the world color everything around him so black that he could not see it for what it was.

"You're a wonderful father, John. And hearing Flora talk about her mother, I know she must have been a fine person. Flora obviously loved her very much."

John looked across at her, glanced back ahead and then said, "Flora was the world to Laura."

It was a surprising conversation for the two of them to be having, considering their past. Considering that just a few weeks ago, neither of them would have imagined ever seeing the other again. Considering that the woman they were discussing had been married to this man with whom Olivia had once thought she would spend the rest of her life.

But then so many things about this weekend had surprised her.

"Care to pick up the pace?" John threw her a look of challenge, his tone lighter, as if he needed to put them back on softer footing.

"I'm game if you are."

He sent Ellie into a nice, easy trot. Olivia gave River a little squeeze with her legs, and they followed, the gait so easy to sit, Olivia actually managed to look as if it hadn't been a decade and a half since she'd been in a saddle.

They went from jog to lope. That easy, Quarter Horse lope, smoother, even, than the jog. They went up a short incline, leveling out onto a straight shot that opened into a clearing where John's grandparents had planted a fruit orchard forty years before.

Olivia's throat tightened. "Oh, John, it's still beautiful."

"You always loved it up here," he said, his voice rimmed with what sounded like the same emotion now squeezing her heart.

Before them stood rows and rows of fruit trees. Apples, peaches, pears. On the far right of those were several arbors of grape vines. The sweet scent in the air was almost intoxicating. "It hasn't changed," she said. "It must be so much work to take care of it."

"Worth it though. I could never let it go," he said, not looking at her.

Could it be that, he, too, cherished the memories they'd made here? Olivia wondered.

"Take a look?" he asked.

She nodded, not trusting her voice.

They dismounted, and John ground-tied both mares. They stood patiently in the way of a well-taught horse, nibbling at the green grass beneath them. John led the way through a row of peach trees, the gnarled old limbs heavy with small to medium-size fruit.

"They should be ready mid-July," he said.

"They smell incredible. What kind?"

"Some yellow. Some white."

"I love the white. They're so sweet."

He sat down against the trunk of one of the old trees. Olivia sat on the grass beside him, and for a little while, they said nothing. They just sat in strangely comfortable, compatible silence, as if neither of them could quite imagine they were actually here in this old retreat together, able to talk about everyday things. It was shocking to Olivia. She realized it didn't pay to think you had too much of this life figured out.

"Tell me about Laura," she said, her voice soft. "Who was she?"

John looked at her, surprise widening his eyes. He dropped his gaze, picked up a twig and rolled it between his palms. He didn't answer for a good while, and just as she was beginning to think she shouldn't have asked, he said, "She was someone who took care of the things life gave her. She loved to read. Usually kept two or three books going. She liked to plant things. Those fig bushes over there," he said, pointing to their left. "She was so proud of getting those things to grow, and the first year they had fruit on them, we had fig everything."

He stopped for a moment, and she waited, wanting to hear more.

"She made these great cakes. Big, tall three-layer things with an inch of icing on top. She was a good woman, a good person. She was sick for a long time."

"That must have been really hard," she said, feeling the insignificance of the words in light of the reality of such a thing.

"It was. For her. For all of us. Wanting to do something to make it different and not being able to do a damn thing."

Olivia put her hand on top of his and squeezed, as if she might soak up some of the pain so obviously still there. "I'm really sorry for what happened to her, John."

"So am I," he said. "Sometimes, I—"

She waited for him to go on, sensed there was some burden in what he was about to say. She removed her hand from his. "Sometimes what?"

"Sometimes, I think I wasn't the husband I should have been," he said, his voice somber. "When you left here, Liv, I never imagined anything could hurt that badly. When I met Laura I guess I was looking for some way to replace you, to make me feel something other than the grief I'd been feeling all those months. I didn't marry her for the right reasons. But from here, from where I sit today, I can't regret any of it. We made a good life together. And Flora—''

''Is everything.''

''She is.''

The guilt in his voice held the weight of steel. Olivia's heart throbbed, for him, for Laura, for all of them. ''You wouldn't have been anything other than a good husband, John.''

''A man ought to be able to start a marriage with a heart that's free and clear of anyone else. I didn't do that.''

Maybe there should have been some satisfaction in knowing that through all these years, he had not forgotten her. But all she felt was sadness, the threads of which were not easily identifiable, entwined as they were with the awareness that another person's life had been affected by the chord that had never been fully severed between John and her.

Because wasn't it true of her own life as well? What she and John had known with one another had been the comparison for every relationship she'd had since.

They sat there a while longer, absorbing, feeling their way forward.

Olivia spoke first. ''I don't know why we end up in the places we do, but there was a reason for you and Laura to be together.''

Another width of silence took up space between them, the sounds of the afternoon standing out in bold relief: the hum of a tractor in the distance, the plaintive moo of a cow calling for a wayward calf.

"I guess I have to believe that, too," he said.

"Your life is what I always pictured it would be. Solid. Stable. You matter. To your family. And to this farm. To me that's what gives a person's days meaning. Knowing that if you weren't here, it would matter, you would be missed. From what I see, Laura's life had meaning. She mattered. She's missed by her family. That's something I envy."

"Why?" he asked, looking surprised.

She shrugged. "Maybe it's just the nature of what I do. There's always someone else waiting to knock you off the ladder. Step over you to get to the next rung."

"Sounds pretty cutthroat."

"It can be."

"Is it what you want to do for the rest of your life?"

"I don't know," she said. "I used to think so. The important thing just seemed to be reaching the next level." She looked down at her lap, smoothed a thumb across the knee of the leather chaps he'd given her to wear. "I'm up for a promotion. A pretty big one, actually. And I'm not sure I want it."

He didn't say anything for a few moments and then, "What do you want, Liv?"

"To matter. To not be expendable." She answered quickly, honesty propelling the words from her.

"Liv, you matter. Good grief, even some of the people we went to school with get tongue-tied around you."

She shook her head. "That's not what I mean."

He studied her for a moment, weighing her words. "People look at someone like you with a life like yours and can't imagine it not being perfect."

"It's not perfect. I've pretty much put work before everything else."

"And now?"

"Now, I keep asking myself what's missing."

"It's easy to spend too much time tending one area of your life. Eventually, the weeds take over the rest, and then all you're left with is that one little well-tended spot."

And that was exactly how Olivia saw her life now. The simple metaphor was John to the heart. He said everything she had been feeling.

"It's been really good spending time with you today, Liv."

A response welled up inside her, uncensored. *I've wanted this for fifteen years. Just an hour with you the way it used to be. I never hoped for an entire day.* But the words were too revealing. So she said, simply, "You, too, John."

They sat a while and let those admissions settle between them.

"Remember that afternoon we rode up here and got caught in a thunderstorm?" There was something like reluctance in his voice, as if this memory led down a road he wasn't sure he wanted to take.

"And our horses decided to go back to the barn without us?"

"Can't say that I blamed them." He smiled.

It had been a horrific storm, lightning flashing in every corner of the sky. Olivia had been terrified, and John had held her tight against him inside the old tool shed at the corner of the orchard. The thunder sounded as if it were right on top of them, and with every clap, she had shivered like a soaked kitten.

She remembered clearly now, John's kiss, his assurance that they would be all right. She'd kissed him back, and they had ended up making love there that late afternoon with the thunder and lightning playing out its symphony around them. And Olivia hadn't been scared anymore, aware that the storm's music was somehow the perfect echo to the feelings of pure love John brought to life inside her.

She looked over at him now, saw that he, too, remembered. It pulled at them. Olivia felt the force of it, knew he would reach for her, thought she might die if he didn't.

His hand found the back of her neck and eased her to him. And when their faces were only inches apart, he looked down at her, his eyes revealing a tumultuous blend of longing and confusion. They were the same emotions at war in her and there was no doubt which would win out. "I'd be a dishonest man if I denied the reason I brought you up here today."

"And what was that?" she asked, her question barely audible.

"For this," he said.

He leaned in and kissed her then.

Olivia forgot to breathe. Forgot everything, except the man next to her and the fact that no one had ever kissed her the way John once had. And it was exactly the same. Except better somehow. Better, maybe, for the loss of all the years that had passed since the last time he'd held her this way. Better, maybe, for the fact that she was in the arms of a man she had once loved, and as a grown woman, knew the potential emptiness of such gestures without the feelings that could accompany them.

Or better, maybe, because they fit, the two of them. This had not changed. Nor had the feelings pulsing upward from her heart, making her chest tighten and her eyes fill up, spill over. They were the kind of feelings that assure a woman there has never been anything like this for her, that there will never again be anything like this with anyone else. The kind of feelings that inspire a twist of elation for the discovery and terror for the potential loss.

John pulled back and rubbed a thumb across each

of her cheeks where the tears had left moist tracks. In the faint light, she could see the questions in his eyes, saw him struggle to voice them.

"Liv," he said, and her name sounded shredded, as if someone had torn it from him. There was pain behind it, and a couple of emotions she couldn't name. He reeled her to him again, not gently this time, but with the very recognizable need of getting her closer, of fitting her to him, which was what she, too, wanted so much that she shook with the possibility of it.

Urgency seized them, raw, unpolished, and they fell back onto the hard ground beneath them, wrapping around one another, into one another, souls reaching, touching.

The kiss was deep, intimate. They changed angles as they searched for better access, mutual need pulling them along as passengers without choice. Because what choice was there in this?

This was full circle; so many times before, they'd come to this place, for privacy, a place to be alone, to be together, to call the world theirs, and theirs alone.

Olivia's hands renewed their knowledge of him, the lean, defined muscles of his back, his shoulders at their widest point, the hair he kept barbershop short. His did the same of her. Down her bare arms, across the dip of her throat, one palm seeking the fullness of her breast, and with a few fluent caresses, siphoning all the strength from her limbs.

And all the while, they kissed with the lack of finesse of two people half their age, neither thinking of anything so levelheaded as reserve or caution or skill. This was chemistry at its most basic, the rare kind that if you're lucky you find once in a lifetime.

"Liv." Her name came with brakes attached. John pulled back, rolled over onto the grass beside her and stared up at the sky, his breathing heavy. She knew where they were headed. That there was a point past which there would be no turning back for either of them.

A string of minutes slid by while they lay there, letting reason regain control.

He reached out, entwined her hand in his, held it up and rubbed her thumb with his. "I loved you so much, Liv."

There was anguish in his voice, questions behind the words. Emotion knotted in her throat, tears blurring the sky above them. He had loved her. Here, now, she felt the truth of it and let it flow through her. All those years ago, she had not trusted that love for what it was. Had not trusted it to protect her, forgive her. That had been her mistake. Because love as strong as theirs had deserved truth. Above all things, it deserved truth.

Didn't she owe him now what she had not given him then? The truth. Even if it did what she had feared it would do all along? Make her forever responsible in his eyes.

She unclasped her hand from his, stood and then moved a few yards away from him, her arms wrapped around her waist. Terror tripped through her, raising her heartbeat so it pounded in her ears. How many times had she played this scene in her mind, how to tell him, what to say? But each of those had merely been rehearsals for a play she had thought would never be staged.

This was the real thing.

He stood behind her. She couldn't bring herself to look at his face, but felt his concern, knew it was there in his eyes.

One more moment, and she might never give in to the fear lashing over her like whitecaps.

"What is it, Liv?" John's voice was low, caring, alarmed.

She tried to answer, but couldn't. The words had been buried for so long that she could hardly find a way to begin.

He waited. She felt that, too. As if he knew this was something that needed its own time.

She clasped her hands together, fixed her gaze on a puffy cloud high in the sky, drew in the sweet scent of the peaches all around them. And said the words. "We were going to have a baby. I was pregnant. I'd only known a week or so—I was so scared I hadn't found the nerve to tell you yet. But I was sick in the mornings, and my dad...he figured out why. He decided to teach me a lesson with a belt one night when he was well on the other side of a bottle of vodka. I lost the baby, John. I lost the baby.''

Olivia heard her own voice, thought it odd that the words sounded as if someone else were saying them. And it felt that way, as if she'd had to numb herself to be able to say them at all.

Around them, birds continued their conversations with one another. One of the mares swished her tail at a fly. Somewhere high above, a jet engine droned. Normal sounds. Life-affirming sounds.

John's hand touched her shoulder, tentative at first, and then sinking in, holding on, as if without her, he might fall. "Liv. Liv."

The anguish in his voice enfolded her heart and squeezed tight. He reached out and pulled her in to him, fast and hard, as if he couldn't get her there quickly enough. He wrapped his arms around her and anchored her to him. Olivia turned her face into his chest and closed her eyes. Here. This was where she'd yearned to be all those years ago. She felt so many things at once, emotions she hadn't allowed anywhere near her heart because it was impossible to live a normal life when she did so. Normal meant smiling and laughing and acting as if her heart had never been broken in half. But here in John's arms, she let the hurt seep up and remembered her anguish, the grief that had only gone dormant, but had never actually died.

That grief wrapped itself around her now, and her shoulders shook with the force of it. She wasn't aware that she was crying until John pulled back. And she saw her own grief mirrored there in his eyes.

She had never seen such pain on a man's face, and her heart broke all over again for the fact that she was responsible for putting it on John's. "I'm sorry," she said. "I wish so much that I had done something...that I could have prevented it from happening."

"Liv. Honey," he said, his voice breaking and then, "What could you have done?"

"Told you sooner. Left home long before then— I don't know. Something."

"Don't." He put a finger to her lips. "You were seventeen years old. I should have been the one to do something. I should have taken care of you—"

"No." She touched the back of her hand to his left cheek. "Don't. I couldn't bear it if you felt guilty over something you never even knew about."

Olivia actually ached for the hurt she knew John was feeling. And at the same time, on another level that had nothing to do with selflessness, there was something freeing in sharing the awful secret with the only other person who had lost as much from it as she had.

"I'd give anything in the world to be able to go back and change it, Liv."

"When I decided to come this weekend, I never intended to tell you this."

"Didn't I have a right to know?"

"I told myself a thousand times it wouldn't change anything. And it won't. You weren't to blame. Then or now."

"How could I not feel responsible?" The words were ragged with emotion.

"We were teenagers. There were things about my life I never told you. You had no way of knowing."

"I should have known," he said. "I should have known." He pulled her to him, tucked her against him and just held her there. The two of them in possession of something that had changed their lives, turned their merged paths in different directions. Forever. Never to be the same.

And there in that old fruit orchard, where the baby that had been theirs was very likely conceived, they held onto each other because that was all they could do.

CHAPTER THIRTEEN

Reckonings

JOHN FELT as if his entire world had been upended.
There was no other way to describe what was going
on inside him. An earthquake of emotions had left
a mile-wide chasm in the center of his heart. A permanent crack that would be as much a part of him
from this point on as the skin that covered his bones.

After they'd ridden the horses back to the house,
he'd driven Liv into town and dropped her off in
front of the bed-and-breakfast. Both of them had
been quiet, as if unsure of what direction to take
with one another, as if what had been said up in that
orchard needed its own time. Even now, disbelief
and truth still felt as if they were sitting on the surface, and like oil and water, they didn't mix.

Liv had been pregnant with his child. And he had
never known.

He felt sore inside, as if he'd been in a bad car
wreck, every inch of him bruised. And at a complete
loss as to what he should be feeling.

In two days the map of everything he'd thought to be true of Liv and himself had been completely redefined, and there wasn't a single place he recognized from this angle.

He turned into the driveway at the farm. Flora waited for him in the front yard, perched on the edge of the wooden swing he'd hung for her from the gnarled limb of an oak tree.

He sat for a moment, one hand on the steering wheel, and watched her.

We were going to have a baby. I was pregnant.

Liv's words came back at him with jagged edges that left him feeling shredded inside.

How could he not have known? How could something that monumental, that important, have taken place without him knowing? How could he have failed to be there for Liv? For the baby? Their baby.

How could something so awful happen to her, and he hadn't known?

Maybe the emotion inside him should have been rage. At her father. At what they had lost. At what had torn them apart.

But all he felt was sadness. Sadness for a child he had never had the chance to know. Sadness for lives that had taken completely different directions than those they'd planned.

And blame. As the boy who had loved Liv, who had made her pregnant, he should have known. He should have known.

A wave of loss swallowed him whole. They could have had a little girl like Flora. Or a little boy. The possibility was a vise on his chest, squeezing, pressing down so hard, all the air left his lungs.

John lunged out of the truck and headed for the swing.

"Daddy, will you push me?" Flora sang out.

"Yep." He stepped behind her, pulled the swing back and then gave it an easy push.

"You smiled a lot today," she said over her shoulder, pumping her legs to make it go higher. "Olivia's nice."

"She is," he said, his voice a note or two off.

"Will she come back to visit us again?"

"I don't know," John said.

"Did she used to be your girlfriend?"

The question startled John enough that he missed a push, and the swing slowed. "Where did you hear that?"

"Sophia said she was."

"A long time ago."

"Is she gonna be again?"

"She doesn't live here anymore."

Silence. John gave the swing another push.

"If you get a girlfriend, will I still be your daughter?"

John stopped the swing, stepped around and picked Flora up, folding her into his arms. "You'll be my daughter forever, baby. Nothing will ever change that. You're a good girl. No daddy could have a better daughter.''

She pulled back and peered up at him through moist eyes. "I'm not always good.''

He ruffled her hair and hugged her again, his heart weighted with love for her and the realization that he did not know what to feel about the loss of a child whose existence would have meant Flora would not be here.

IN HER ROOM, Olivia got in the shower, leaving the water on cool as if the shock of it might jolt some of the confusion inside her into some kind of certainty that telling John the truth had been the right thing.

Had it?

She dropped her head back and let the water sluice down her face.

She didn't know what to make of the awkwardness between them when they had parted earlier. He'd dropped her off outside Lavender House with a casual, "See you tonight, Liv." As if he'd needed to put emotional distance between them again.

But then what did she expect?

Olivia had no idea what the outcome of finally telling John the truth would be. Whether, as she had always feared, he would end up feeling she could somehow have prevented what had happened. Or whether they might both be able to put it to rest, with sorrow that would forever preface thoughts of what might have been, but also with acceptance of the fact that sometimes the world brought to a person's doorstep things that were unfair.

Olivia did not regret coming here this weekend. Even after all these years, this trip back had brought her own healing to another level. One of realization. She finally accepted that she had done nothing to deserve what had happened to her.

She, Olivia Ashford, had been a victim. And for the first time in her adult life, she let the word sink in, take root.

A victim then, yes. But no more. She would not spend the rest of her life as prisoner to her past. To do so would be to allow what had happened all those years ago to have final say. Telling John today had been the most crucial step out of that cage.

A little door had opened inside her, and light came through the small crack. Always, her past had occupied a dark part of herself. She'd kept it closed up and sealed tight. There had been purpose in opening it today, her need to give John the truth, at last. But maybe there was something more, too.

Maybe it was time to turn what was left of the bad into something good.

MICHAEL ARRIVED at Olivia's room just after five-thirty.

She opened the door, wishing now that she had insisted he not come.

"Hi," he said, leaning in to peck her cheek.

"Hi. Have you already checked in?"

He nodded. "Showered and ready to go."

"Bet you're tired."

"No, actually," he said, stepping past her into the room. "I napped on the plane."

"I hate that you came all this way just for one night."

"I'm not. So tell me about it. You haven't fallen in love with any old boyfriends, have you?"

Olivia threw him a startled glance and saw that he was teasing. "Ah, it's been good. I'm really glad I came."

He sank down in the wingback chair in the corner of the room. "So have you thought any more about the promotion?"

"A little."

"I'm surprised you can sleep for thinking about it."

Olivia glanced at her watch, deliberately skirting the subject, and realized that she'd actually thought very little about it. "We should probably head on over if you're ready."

"At your disposal," he said.

During the drive out to Rolling Hills, he talked about work, what had been going on since she'd left Thursday morning. And it was like hearing about someone else's life. She felt removed from it, as if it didn't belong to her.

She forced herself to respond at the appropriate points in their conversation, answering his questions on how everything had gone so far, but her mind was elsewhere, at a picnic table beside a country diner, in the front seat of a Dodge truck, under an old peach tree with achingly familiar arms around her.

At the farm they got out, and it felt more than a little strange walking up the driveway with Michael. No sooner had she made the admission than another one made itself known. She cared what John would think when he saw them.

"Beautiful place," Michael said.

"It is."

Lori was waiting at the edge of the yard. She waved and weaved her way through several people, a welcoming smile on her face. "Hello," she said, sticking out her hand. "You must be Michael. Olivia said you were coming."

He smiled. "I am. I did."

"Michael, this is Lori," Olivia said. "My best friend for longer than either of us wants to admit."

They talked for a few minutes and Michael complimented the reunion set-up. He had a way of putting others immediately at ease, and Olivia could see that Lori was pleased by his comments.

"Well, he seems like a nice guy," she said when

Michael went to get them a bottle of water from one of the coolers across the yard. "Just friends, huh?"

"Very nice. And yes, just friends."

Lori led her to a couple of chairs positioned beside a crape myrtle bush. "So where were you all day?"

It was hard to miss the hopeful note in her friend's voice. Olivia thought about telling Lori everything then. What had happened all those years ago. The fact that she'd just told John today. But not yet. The secret had been hers for fifteen years. It seemed right to let John have it to himself a while longer.

"I think being here has made me remember parts of who I used to be, who I wanted to be," she said now. "And maybe I've realized that it's okay to still want some of that."

Lori reached out and squeezed her hand, the simple gesture one of understanding. And Olivia thought how nice it was to have a best friend again.

"STANDS OUT like a sore thumb, doesn't he?"

John and Cleeve were standing in the hamburger line. John was trying not to look in the direction of either Liv or the man who'd arrived with her an hour earlier. "Big-shot producer," Cleeve had announced a couple of minutes before, having garnered his information from Zelda Ayers who'd heard it from Thomasa Conroy.

Illogical as it was, a stun gun couldn't have had

more of an effect on John than Liv showing up with someone tonight. It was the last thing he'd expected. Jealousy burned inside him like a hot coal.

But then what had he thought? That she didn't date? That she'd lived a life of celibacy since she'd left here?

The truth was he hadn't thought about it. Hadn't let himself then and didn't want to get anywhere near it now.

But he was human, and he couldn't help taking a long look at the man. He could have stepped out of the front window of some fancy men's department store. His clothes had a different look to them from those of most of the other men at the picnic supper. He was wearing some kind of fancy golf shirt, the kind that cost a hundred and fifty dollars or better and linen shorts with a crease so sharp John could have sliced his hamburger bun with it. His haircut wasn't the barbershop kind like John's, but clearly said seventy-five dollars or more.

Despite the fashion statement, he made short work of putting himself out in the middle of the crowd. He moved from group to group, talking to people, smiling and nodding at things John was sure he must have little, if any, interest in. And all the while his eyes kept going back to Liv who was talking to Lori over by the drink table.

John couldn't keep his own gaze from straying in that direction. She looked incredible tonight. Her hair was up in some sort of twist that was somehow both sexy and innocent. His hands itched to pull out the pins holding it in place and tangle his fingers in its fullness.

Seeing her with another man tonight was like being punched in the stomach. It brought him to the full-blown realization that somewhere deep inside him, despite his own need to find footing with it, he had begun to think of everything that had happened today as a beginning, as a turning point that might somehow hold sway with the future.

"You're in love with her again, aren't you?"

Cleeve's assertion was issued with uncharacteristic quiet, although there was no missing the certainty in his voice.

"It's not that simple, Cleeve."

"Not too many things are. But hell, John, for whatever reason—and I believe there is a reason because I'm a man who happens to think the guy upstairs knows what he's doing—you and Liv went your separate ways. But if something is meant to be between the two of you, why can't it just start with now instead of with then?"

John thought of all that Cleeve didn't know and wondered if any of it actually changed the basic truth of what he'd just said.

"You and me," Cleeve fishtailed a hand between them, "our roads have been a little different, but from where I stand, it looks like we could both end up with a missed-out banner draped across our front porch. And I'm beginning to think I don't wanna be one of those guys.''

John threw another glance at the man Liv had brought with her tonight. He didn't want to be one of those guys, either. He had to talk to her. And suddenly, he couldn't wait another minute.

''OH, SHOOT.'' Racine held her small, inexpensive-looking camera on end, glancing up to find Cleeve standing in front of her, studying her with amused eyes.

''So how many pictures are you plannin' on taking this weekend?''

''Enough for a scrap book,'' she said. ''Guess you think that's silly.''

''Nope. Don't see anything silly about it at all.''

''Well, the end's going to be missing. My batteries are dead.''

''Then we better get the lady some more. Can't have an unfinished scrapbook. Come on,'' he said, taking her by the hand. ''The minute market down the road should have some.''

The obvious answer was thanks, but no thanks. Before coming over here tonight, Racine had made herself promise that she would keep her distance from Cleeve Harper. But that resolution was becoming harder and harder to stick to. Being around Cleeve was like having your very own clown, Labrador retriever and fan club all wrapped up in the same package. He'd complimented her outfit earlier tonight—a dress she'd had for years—as if he meant it, with a look in his eyes that made her cheeks flush with color.

And not to mention that he was so darn good-looking.

Racine had always had a thing for guys in cowboy hats.

Really, Macy Harper had no idea what she had.

So what harm could there be in driving with him to the minute market? She did need the batteries. She had no intention of changing her resolve. He was married. Married! But it would only take a few minutes. How much trouble could a girl get into in that amount of time?

They headed out to Cleeve's truck, walking side by side down the driveway. His arm brushed hers. Racine took a quick step sideways, trying to look inconspicuous and failing entirely.

"I don't bite," he said.

"Not what I heard," she shot back, sounding more flip than she felt.

He chuckled. "A man likes to think he's still dangerous."

She laughed. "Oh, you're dangerous, all right."

He opened the truck door, waited for her to climb in, then shut it behind her. Manners, too. This had better be a quick trip.

Cleeve got in, started the truck up, and they rolled down the driveway. They were quiet at first, in the way of two people who are attracted to one another and shouldn't be, the silence bearing weight, implication.

And so Racine filled it with chatter, inane, meaningless stuff that made him look at her with a smile that told her he knew exactly what she was doing.

He reached out and flipped on the radio. Tim McGraw was singing one of those songs that make a woman's blood heat up.

"Can't you find something else on that radio?" she asked, lifting her hair off the back of her neck.

Cleeve looked over at her and grinned. "So what's wrong with this?"

"The theme's all wrong," she said, flipping the dial to a station known for its elevator music, the kind that was as bland as soup out of a can.

He looked across at her, with an eyebrow raised in acknowledgment of her mood-buster choice. "So why didn't we ever get together in high school?"

"Probably because I wasn't the kind of girl you would have gotten together with."

"What kind's that?"

"The kind that didn't have inch-thick glasses or wear her hair in pigtails."

"Well, somewhere along the way, you sure did figure it out."

Unwise though she knew it to be, Racine let the

compliment wash over her, warm places inside her that had been long ago convinced there must be something wrong with her. How else could she have ended up with a man who thought it perfectly fine to use her as his own personal punching bag?

Cleeve let off the gas and hit his blinker.

Racine sat up in the seat. "Why are you turning here?"

"Just taking a short cut."

"I don't think we should go this way," she said.

"Why? You know about a roadblock or something?"

"No. I'd just rather go the other way."

"This'll be a little faster. Gotta get you back so you can finish taking all your pictures."

"Cleeve, really, I—" Maybe she was being paranoid. He'd said Macy had gone to visit her sister. There was no reason to think she'd be anywhere near here.

The house was a quarter mile or so ahead on the right. Racine started talking again, about farming and cows, the words coming out at roller-coaster speed. If she talked fast enough, maybe he wouldn't even look that way.

They were almost at the mailbox. Racine threw a panicked glance at the driveway. Sure enough, there was Macy's car. Parked out front bold as daylight. That woman didn't have the good sense God gave a turnip—

Cleeve slammed on the brakes, and the truck came to a tire-smoking stop.

"What are you doing?" she asked, trying not to look at the car.

But he was.

"What the hell?" Cleeve threw the truck in reverse, backing up at a good thirty miles an hour.

"Cleeve—"

He stopped the truck right in front of the house. Stared at the car for a long, agonizing minute. And then looked at Racine. "You knew, didn't you?"

How could she lie? The fact that Macy Harper was having an affair with Joe Billings was no secret. After seeing the two of them ogling each other in the post office one day, Racine had wondered if the woman just wanted to get caught.

"Cleeve, I—"

He threw the truck in gear and roared off down the road, not letting her finish. She let him drive too fast for a good five miles, figuring he needed to let off a little steam.

"You know, I'm not too keen on the thought of dying tonight," she said finally.

"Shit." He slammed a palm against the steering wheel, letting off the gas. The truck slowed to the speed limit.

"Pull over, Cleeve," she said, reaching out and putting a hand on his arm. "Let's just sit for a minute."

Another mile or two slid by before he smacked on the signal and whipped the truck over to the side of the road.

"So who else knows? The whole damn county?"

The pain in his voice made Racine's heart twist. "Are you really worried about that?"

"Why didn't you tell me?"

"Because it wasn't my place to do so."

"I thought we were friends."

"If I'd told you that, you wouldn't have thought so. And besides, you might have suspected my motives."

He considered that for a moment. "I guess it's not the kind of thing that's real easy to bring up. Hey, Harper, your wife sure does visit her sister a lot."

"Cleeve."

"I must look like a damn fool."

"You don't look like any such thing. If Macy only knew—"

"What?"

"You're a good man. She's the one missing out."

He cupped a hand to his forehead and squeezed his eyes shut. "I'm pathetic," he said. "Looking the other way all this time when I knew something wasn't right."

"Sometimes people just don't end up being who we thought they were," she said. "I can say that from firsthand experience. And besides, I can one-up you on pathetic.''

He looked up at her. ''I doubt that.''

''I came to this reunion this weekend all set to snag a great guy. Funny thing is I ended up renewing my crush on this cowboy who's completely unavailable.''

Cleeve threw her a startled look, and then blew out a sigh. A small smile touched the corner of his very appealing mouth. ''You're just saying that because I've been cuckolded.''

She laughed. ''I've never known a man who would even know how to use the word.''

''You mean would have needed to.''

''I've known plenty,'' she said, putting her hand over his.

He had on a short-sleeve shirt, and his skin felt cool to her touch, as if the shock of what he'd just seen had chilled his blood. She wanted to warm him up again, wrap her arms around him and wipe that look from his eyes forever.

Though she had not spoken a word, she had no doubt her feelings showed clearly on her face. Racine didn't bother to hide them. She figured it would do him good to know.

''Racine—''

The tone of his voice held warning. She would have been wise to heed it. But good heavens, she really did want him to kiss her. Once. Just once.

He leaned toward her, closing up the space between them. Then he sank his mouth onto hers in
the kind of kiss that brands a woman for life. A kiss
that makes her feel as if her very bones might dis-
solve. A kiss that begins with the clear purpose of
making it impossible for her to say no.

Racine slid her hands up his chest, locked them
around his neck and kissed him back. Full and deep
without a smidge of the reserve that should have
been there.

Cleeve groaned and half pulled, half lifted her
across the seat so that she was nearly sitting on his
lap. "Racine."

A woman could wait her whole life to hear her
name said like that. Racine had. No man had ever
uttered her name with the kind of need that was in
Cleeve's voice now. Her own attraction to him
fought an admirable battle with her conscience. It
would have been so easy to give in and just enjoy
being wanted this way. But then tomorrow would
come, and she'd have to listen to her own regrets.
Because starting something with Cleeve Harper on
a night like this would do nothing but guarantee its
certain demise.

She pulled back with toothpick-weak resolve.
"Not like this, Cleeve. You don't know how much
I'd like to say yes, but not like this."

He let her go, sat back in his seat and drew in a

couple of deep breaths. "Guess we better get those batteries, huh?"

"You're going to be all right, Cleeve. Really, you are."

And in the dim light of the truck's interior, his eyes told her that, more than anything, he wanted to believe her.

CHAPTER FOURTEEN

Spring's Touch

OLIVIA FORCED HERSELF to walk across the dew-damp grass to the pond behind John's house. She'd been helping Lori write down orders for the group picture a photographer had shot after dinner when John had come up behind her and asked, close to her ear, if she would meet him in fifteen minutes. They needed to talk.

There were a thousand reasons for her not to go. But she could not turn back. It was simply not within her ability to do so. She'd left Michael at the other end of the yard, trying to fix a problem at work from his cell phone.

It was dark by the water's edge; there were no lights along the narrow dock, only the shadows thrown out from the party going on at the house behind them.

"Liv?"

"It's me," she said, a sudden fist of nerves nailing her to the spot.

John appeared out of the darkness in front of her and put a steadying hand on her arm. "Careful, it's hard to see out here."

She was glad if it gave him a reason to touch her. He held onto her until they'd reached the farthest point of the dock. Their stiff postures screamed the sudden awkwardness between them: he with hands now shoved in the pockets of his jeans; she with arms clasped around herself. The music from the reunion had started up again, the bass throbbing out a seductive beat.

"Do you want to sit down?" John said, uncertainty leaving footprints on the words.

Olivia nodded. They sat, close enough that their shoulders touched, their feet hanging just above the pond's surface.

Frogs talked all around them. A breeze tiptoed by, lifting the strands of Olivia's hair.

He planted his hands on the edge of the dock, his gaze pointed at the water beneath their feet. "Liv, I—"

"John, I—"

These beginnings were said in unison.

"Go ahead," he said.

"No, you, really."

"A week ago, no one could ever have convinced me that you and I—"

"—would ever speak to one another again?"

"Pretty much."

. "I don't think I would have believed it, either. But I'm glad I was wrong."

"So am I."

Quietly issued, the admission sent a shiver through her. How many times in the past fifteen years had she imagined such a scene between the two of them? Heard such words in daydreams that played on into the night? Told herself it was the only place she would ever again hear them?

But this wasn't a dream.

And he had really said that.

A good stretch of silence, and then, "What you told me this afternoon…it's a lot to take in after so many years."

"I know."

"I feel like I lost something I never knew I had."

"I'm sorry." And she was. More than she could ever express with words.

"But it wasn't your fault." He looked at her then, moonlight illuminating the pain on his face. She could have spared him that. Sometimes, there was something to be said for not knowing.

"Maybe I should have left it alone, John. There was nothing to be changed by my telling you. It's all in the past now."

"There was everything to be changed," he said, and something in his voice sent a shiver skidding down her spine. "And the fact that you and I conceived a child together will be with me for the rest of my life. It will never be in the past.''

Emotion welled inside her, pure and true. Tears slid down her cheeks. She couldn't stop them and didn't try. She looked up, let him see her grief. It was still there, would never be, as he had said, a thing of the past. ''I decided a long time ago that God sends us on certain paths for a reason. I have to believe that what happened was meant to be. All of it. That He had another purpose for our child other than life on this earth.''

''Liv,'' he said, the sound of her name carrying an echo of his own grief. He reached for her, pulled her to him, and they held one another, anchors, each.

It felt as if they had reached some mutual place where it was possible for them to put to rest the things they could not change. Accept the roads their lives had led them down. And she was glad for this crossing of paths. There was no way to know the outcome. But she was grateful for the moment—this weekend, if that was all it could be—for the gift that it was.

They sat there on the old dock, night enveloping them.

John pulled back, looked down at her, brushed the back of his hand across her cheek, the tenderness of the gesture bringing a confusion of feeling surging up from her heart. She reached down, slipped off her sandals, let her feet dip into the night-cool water. "Mmm, that feels good."

John dipped his hand in and let the water trickle through his fingers. "Some of those guppies down there have teeth."

She popped her feet from the water, pink-tipped toes gleaming in the moonlight. "Remember when we used to swim here, and those little fish would dart up and take a nibble?"

"I remember that polka-dot bathing suit you had that they seemed to like pretty well."

Olivia smiled.

"And I remember that seeing you in it nearly drove me out of my hormone-enraged mind."

Now she laughed. And it felt good remembering those times. Talking about them out loud. Recalling her own disbelief that a boy like John Riley had been crazy about her. He had. And what a feeling that had been. Heady, intoxicating.

It was the same now. That part didn't change with age. She could feel the warm longing emanating from him as if she had sensors attached to her skin, making her attuned to this man's needs, and his alone.

He needed her. She knew somewhere deep inside where her own need still flared.

Proof came when he reached out, bracketed both her legs with one arm, placed them across his lap, the feel of his jeans provocative against her bare skin.

Olivia could not speak, her words smothered by a sudden blanket of heat.

His hand, the palm rough with calluses, made long, stroking motions down the length of her calf. "Still so soft," he said, shaking his head as if the discovery amazed him. "When I was a boy, I knew girls were different. They just looked like they were made up of other stuff than we were. But the first time I ever touched you, I was sure God must have spun you from silk."

The words went straight to her heart. "John," she said, letting the palm of her own hand find his face, brushing her knuckles across skin just slightly rough with stubble. She ached, literally ached, from the contrast.

"So...you're seeing somebody? The guy with you tonight?" Surprising as they were, the questions were strained, as if they were hard for him to say, as if he did not want to ask, but had to know.

"Friends. We used to be more. He was trying to do me a favor by coming."

She felt John's relief. Welcomed it.

They looked at each other, simply looked, with what felt to Olivia like the need to take one another in, brand their consciousness with the fact that they were really here together, when only so recently, the possibility had not existed. The feelings inside her had the kind of roots that only develop after years of enduring the worst of hardships, drought, winter's cold. Surviving and all the stronger for it, their grip on life firmer than before. Thriving with spring's touch. Bringing to full, blossoming life everything she'd once felt for him. Still felt for him.

He leaned in and kissed her then. His mouth warm and intent on hers. And it was like picking up where they'd left off. From this afternoon. From so many years before. The feelings the same and yet laced now with something different. Tenderness. Olivia felt it in his touch. Palpable understanding of why they had taken the paths they'd taken. And regret, too. For everything they had lost. *They* had lost. This was the difference in what she felt now. As if she were no longer out on the life raft alone. John was with her. Together, they would stay afloat. Because if their future went no further than this night, she knew she would never again be alone with the loss she'd carried herself for so long. She had seen, clearly, on John's face that he felt it, too.

Nothing in her life had ever felt as right as this. The kind of right that is soul deep. But hadn't everything with John started there? From the knowledge that he was the one? That for her there would never be another. Not like this.

He turned, angling his thigh on the dock and pulling her into the wedge of space between his legs. His arms circled her waist and held her there as if the thought of ever letting her go could not possibly exist. Then the kiss shifted in momentum, from tenderness to something raw and urgent. With one swift motion, he slid her backward, one arm cushioning the back of her head against the dock.

She maintained presence of mind enough to focus on a few things: how absolutely rock-solid he was against her; how for the first time in her adult life she felt the power a woman knows when a man wants her the way John wanted her now. And this, too: she wanted it to last forever.

His hand found the hem of her shirt, slipped under to reacquaint itself with her waist, the flat of her stomach, and then upward to the round of her breast. Olivia's own hands went to the buttons of his shirt and undid the top four.

John's leg wedged between hers, pressing into her with the kind of purpose that does not require words for definition. And they kissed as they had when they'd been teenagers, without thought of consequence, but only with the intent of making peace with the need demanding acknowledgement inside them. Amazing, she thought with hazy awareness, that it could still be like that. The most pleasurable thing she'd ever known, and at the same time, nearly excruciating in its quest for completion.

Voices sounded somewhere close by.

Olivia and John went still, but remained where they were, hands joined.

"I'm sure she just went for a walk or something." Lori's voice. "She's probably already back at the house. Why don't we go see?"

"All right." Michael. "But if she's not there—"

The rest of the sentence faded out and blended in with the music from the reunion.

Olivia sat up. John followed.

She took in a few calming breaths. Counted some stars. Searched out the Milky Way. Sanity returned, unwelcome though it was.

"Would you have come out here if you'd known that was going to happen?"

His question brought a stop to her galaxy search. "I would have come sooner."

She felt his smile in the darkness. And sensed, although he did not speak, that he was pleased with her answer. The frogs carried on a couple more lengthy conversations while they studied the sky with the intensity of career astronomers.

"I'd better go," she said.

"Yeah, I guess so."

She got up, smoothed a hand across her skirt, tried to right her blouse, which was seriously askew. Her hair had come down, the barrette nowhere in sight.

"We've got a mare due to foal any minute," John said, his voice low, urgency in its threads. "Hank stayed at the barn last night so it's my turn to stay tonight. Meet me there, Liv. Please."

That word, raw, vulnerable, hung between them

with all its implications. Maybe someone younger than she, more naive than she, could have told herself they could meet again in a couple of hours and not finish what they had started here. But if she went, she would be going under the full knowledge that denying their need its conclusion was likely beyond their very human capability.

MICHAEL DID NOT ASK where she had been when Olivia found him talking with Lori's husband, Sam, a few minutes later. He did not mention the fact that he had been looking for her.

He stayed by her side for the rest of the night. People began to leave around eleven. There were lots of hugs, promises to stay in touch. Olivia exchanged addresses with several old friends, hugged Lori and told her she would come by in the morning before she left. She and Michael walked to the car in silence.

"So there was an old boyfriend, right?" Michael said once they were on the road back to town, his voice holding an unexpectedly serious note.

"I didn't mean to be dishonest with you," she said. "It's kind of complicated."

He gave her a long look. "You know being here isn't about anything real. Going back to the place where we grew up is always seductive. But it's not real. Real for you is D.C. and a career that's about to go into overdrive."

His words echoed inside her, the career he referred to a lot like cotton candy, pretty to look at, the first few bites delicious, but in reality it was lighter than air, and it got way too sweet before it was all gone.

"I'm not sure that's what I want anymore. This weekend has been about so many things for me. Most of all, it's made me look at where I've been, something I've spent a lot of years avoiding. But I think I finally realized that looking back is the only way to figure out how to go forward. And that's what I want to do now."

Michael parked the car in front of the bed-and-breakfast. He killed the engine and said, "Olivia, it's perfectly understandable for a weekend like this to make you think about things that used to be, maybe even what might have been. But when you leave here, there will only be what actually is."

"You may be right, Michael."

"So. If I've been harboring any hopeful misconceptions about the two of us ever being more than friends again, I should go ahead and put those away now." He gave her a rueful smile.

She reached across, put her hand on his and squeezed. "Thank you for coming. I'm sorry I was such a lousy date."

He dropped his head back against the seat and laughed. "The worst in memory. And that's saying something."

Olivia smiled.

"I'll catch an earlier flight back in the morning."

"Make it up to you?"

"I'll hold you to it."

CHAPTER FIFTEEN

Imprints

OLIVIA PARKED outside the barn and went inside where the smell of alfalfa hay perfumed the air with its warm, earthy smell. Soft light shone from beneath a stall door halfway down the center aisle. She walked toward it, heart pounding.

John was inside the stall, his back to her. "Hi," she said, keeping her voice low.

He turned around. "You came," he said, genuine pleasure in his eyes. The recognition of it lit something inside Olivia, something warm and tender and good.

He beckoned her forward. "Not all mares are as nice as this one about sharing their babies, but she's enjoying showing the little guy off, I think."

Olivia stepped inside the stall. The floor was deeply bedded with straw. Curled up in front of them lay a newborn foal, chestnut with a white blaze down the center of its face. The mare stood above, licking her baby's soft coat clean.

"Oh, John," Olivia said, one hand to her chest. "Are they all right?"

"Pretty much perfect as far as I can tell. The mare's name is Celia. Her son doesn't have a name yet."

Celia gave the foal a tender nudge with her nose as if to say, "Get up now. Try out your new legs." But the baby wasn't ready yet, from all appearances still exhausted from the effort of finding his way into the world. The bond between the two was already apparent, and the reality of it touched Olivia deeply.

"Stay right here," he said. "I'll be back."

He was gone just seconds, and then he was back with a box containing a curious assortment of things: a plastic bag, brushes, clippers, a towel.

"What is all that for?" she asked.

"Imprinting. Something we started doing a few years ago. It was developed by an equine vet named Robert Miller. The theory is that newborn foals can be desensitized to noises and objects in the first hour or so of their lives. In other words, if you rub plastic all over their bodies now and get them to accept it, they'll never be afraid of it."

"And it really works?"

"We've had amazing results with it. The babies we've been able to imprint soon after they're born are far easier to handle and just seem to be people-horses from the beginning."

Olivia watched, mesmerized, as he began carefully rubbing a towel over the baby's ears, face, shoulders. The foal struggled at first, but John's touch was gentle, persistent.

"The idea is to push past their resistance," he said. "If I stopped rubbing while he was resisting, then that would tell him struggling made me stop doing what I'm doing. So I continue the action until he gives in to it, and then I stop."

Celia whinnied, the first worry she had shown at their presence.

"It's okay, girl," John reassured her. "I'm not going to hurt him. He's just getting a few early lessons, that's all."

With his words, or maybe just the sound of his voice, the mare seemed to relax.

John reached for a pair of clippers, turned them on and let them run for a few seconds, then touched them to the foal. The vibration startled him, and he tried to get up. But John continued to softly rub them against the baby until he stopped struggling and accepted their presence as something non-threatening. "Let's see if he'll try to stand now."

John offered Olivia a hand and they got to their feet, backing up to give the foal room. They waited a few moments; he struggled to get up, almost made it, then fell back down.

Olivia glanced at John, concerned.

"He's okay." He reached out and touched her arm. His hand slid down to find hers, enclosing it in his warm grip. Something inside Olivia took wing and flew. And they stood there together while the baby tried once more to get up, and this time stood before them on seriously quaking legs, but he was standing. Olivia and John couldn't stop smiling, and the mare's gentle nudge of her foal said, "There, you did it."

It was a remarkable sight to witness, and Olivia's eyes grew moist. "Did you know she was going to have the baby tonight?"

John shook his head. "She was already four days late. They do their best to foal when no one is looking."

"I'll never forget this," she said.

He had finished putting away the items he'd brought into the stall. He looked at her now, eyes serious in the shadowed light. "I'm glad you came, Liv. To be honest, I wasn't sure you would."

The words were layered with meaning, and Olivia wanted to freeze frame them, take them apart, replay each one.

The foal had steadied on his feet, and he moved toward his mother now, his nose instinctively searching out sustenance. He found the mare's milk easily enough, this particular obstacle far less difficult for him than getting to his feet.

John reached down and picked up the box. "Why don't we let them have a little time to get to know one another?"

Olivia followed him out into the aisle. He put the box down and slid the door closed. The click of the latch was loud in the silence of the barn. Or maybe it was simply Olivia's own alertness to the man beside her, attuned as she was to his every gesture, every move.

"John, I—" she began, with no idea where the words were going, knowing only that the awareness between them, both physical and emotional, was acute and demanded acknowledgment.

"Liv."

She looked up at him there in the dusky light of the barn and found herself unable to say anything. Because how could words begin to express the feelings in her heart? He had once been a boy for whom her love had known no bounds. Now, here, tonight, he was a man for whom that old attraction had taken on new shape, new dimension. Now she was attracted to the man he had become. A caring father. A man with a heart for animals. A man to whom friendship was a garden worth tending.

She felt the melding of the two, old with new, forging together to become stronger than they might ever have been as one.

"I don't know if I've ever wanted anything more in my life than I want to kiss you right now," John said.

She turned her face to his. "So what are you waiting for?"

He smiled, and it was a good moment during which a lot of things were said, none needing words for expression. He reached out and touched her cheek with the back of a work-roughened hand. Olivia closed her eyes and savored the feel of it, wanted to draw it out, draw upon it. When she looked up again and met his gaze, she saw a reflection of her own feelings there, need and wanting, the intensity of it more than a little terrifying.

His hand went to the back of her neck, his fingers slipping into her hair, then wrapping round it as if he needed some means of steadying himself, of holding on. And at the same time, he bent toward her, his mouth seeking and finding hers. It was a kiss worth waiting for. Magic. Warm, electric. It lit her up from somewhere deep inside, sent currents of feeling surging upward, outward. Somewhere, in the back of her mind, Olivia thought, if a woman could only have one kiss in her lifetime, it should be a kiss like this, one that made her feel that for this man, she was the only woman in the world.

John pulled back and studied her face. Breathing had become something she had to think about; his carried the same uneven edge.

His hand followed the curve of her shoulder to her bare arm, lingering at her forearm before moving down and closing round her hand, his fingers entwining with hers, his eyes asking a silent question to which hers gave acquiescence.

He guided her into a room that looked like an office. There was a leather sofa here, a wooden chair and desk, some photos on the wall, John as a boy with show horses, John as a man, ribbons and trophies in a bookcase.

He closed the door, sealing them in. A narrow strip of moonlight shone through the window behind the desk and, for a moment, divided them.

Olivia looked up, found his gaze on her face, and knew the swell of power a woman feels when a man looks at her with absolute, undiluted longing, as if she is his other half, his reflection.

John stepped into the strip of moonlight then and kissed her, long and full. Their heads tilted, found the right angle, and the kiss deepened, slow, heavy, sweet. It would be forever imprinted upon her memory in the same way each of the things John had exposed the newborn foal to would be forever imprinted upon his. For the rest of her life, she'd be changed, never to be the same.

The room smelled of well-kept leather, and it was quiet except for the rustle of their clothing, his jeans against her cotton dress, and the soft sounds of a man and woman seeking closeness—needing it to breathe, to continue existing.

"You feel so good."

"I've missed this."

"I never thought—"

"Me, either."

"Liv…"

"John…"

Their words hung there, needing no finish, their meaning and the feeling behind them clear. And they kissed—long, slow kisses filled with emotion: regret, joy, yearning and undiluted desire, simple in its honesty, in its inability to disguise itself as anything other than what it was. John fitted her closer to him, curved her into his arms. And all the years that had passed between now and the last time he'd held her like this melted away.

His mouth found the sensitive spot on her neck, and a shiver skittered up her back.

"It's still there." He leaned back to meet her eyes.

"What?"

"That place where it tickles when I kiss you."

Olivia smiled because he had remembered and because there had never been another man who knew her better than this one. There'd never been a man she had ever *let* know her better than this one.

The next kiss, when it came, was softer, more gentle, and there was hesitancy attached. Her arms made brackets between John's shoulder blades, and she let them slide down to his waist, pulling back far enough that she could see his face. "What is it?"

He laced his fingers through hers and placed their joined hands in the center of his chest. And she felt the pounding of both their hearts, eager and not a little scared. He shook his head. "You're just…beautiful. So beautiful, Liv."

She kissed him then, emotion filling her heart to the brim, spilling over.

Here, now, Olivia understood that love was sunshine and rain, that it made things bloom. And she understood what it was to be made for someone. To have a heart that opens for one person only, bleeds for one person only. She knew what it was to have skin that burned beneath the touch of that one person, a body that yearned to be held by that one person.

For her, that had once been John. It was still John. And for as long as she lived would always be John.

There in the dark of the small barn office, with a puddle of moonlight at their feet, he made love to her with his mouth, his hands and his words, every gesture, every touch defining the very meaning of the phrase. They pulled clothes from one another, their motions urgent with need. She unbuttoned his cotton shirt, slid it from his shoulders with both hands, and warmth welled up while her eyes took pleasure in just looking at him. To her, he was perfection, from the work-sculpted muscles of his shoulders, arms, chest, to the point where the top of her head met the dip of his throat.

He unzipped her dress, dropped it to her waist and made a low sound of appreciation as his gaze took its fill of her.

He dropped an arm and swooped her up against him, carried her over to the leather sofa against the far wall of the room. He laid her down, and even the single moment of separation was more than Olivia could stand. She reached for him, pulled him down to her and was glad for the sudden weight of him. This too, was new, and yet, not. She had not forgotten the feel of him this way. The pleasurable heaviness of his body on hers.

And there, in those very basic surroundings with the very basic needs of a man and woman seeking to fill empty places, they gave to one another with the kind of selflessness that in its honesty is human nature at its best. It was as if this night might permanently heal the scars of the past with the sure and certain rhythm of love expressed in its simplest, most perfect form.

HE COULD SPEND the rest of his life just watching her sleep. Just holding her, his senses forever stamped with her sweet scent.

Liv had curled up against him on the too-short sofa, her expression soft and trusting. She slept deeply, peacefully.

She made a little snuffling noise, shifted, then angled closer against him, her naked body bringing his out of its drowsiness. He tightened his arms around her, tucked his chin into the curve of her neck.

Dear God, he'd never imagined feeling like this

again. Wanting like this. Needing so badly that a place way down inside him, a place that felt like his soul, actually ached with it.

As a boy, these were the feelings he had known with Liv. Despite his youth, he'd known the magnitude of them then. He'd realized that it must be rare to know such a connection with another human being. But now as a man, his appreciation for the rarity of it went beyond what he could even find words to describe.

Making love to Liv had been like going back, traveling a familiar road to a much-loved place and realizing once you got there that memory had failed in the recollection of detail. It had failed to recall the softness of her hair and the way he had once loved the feel of it brushing his chest when she bent to kiss him. It had failed to remember the soft sound that came from some equally soft spot inside her when he touched her.

But maybe that was all that had saved him in losing her fifteen years ago, the fading away of such details.

He had no illusions that anything about this night would ever fade from his mind. He was a man now, and she was a woman who unlocked all things for him. Love had trickled through from the past and roared through him now in a river at its banks.

Where do we go from here, Liv? Can there be

*more than this? Will you want more? Will I lose you
all over again? Could I survive that?*

The questions did not come with answers. And
their sharp edges kept him awake, afraid to sleep,
afraid to miss even a moment of this unexpected
gift.

SUNLIGHT DUCKED its head inside the room.

Olivia awoke with reluctance, stretched one arm
above her head, midsection arched, aware even before full reality settled upon her that this was how
she would wish to wake up every morning for the
rest of her life were she given the choice.

John had ended up on the inside of the couch, his
sleeping position one of half-sitting because his legs
were too long. He had both arms around her bare
waist; her face was against his chest, and she had
tucked herself into him as if it was where she belonged.

Which was exactly how it felt.

"Are you awake?"

His voice was night-roughened, and just hearing
it made her curl more deeply into his embrace. He
made a sound that did not exist as a word in the
English vocabulary, but which she understood all
the same, aimed as it was at letting her know her
movement brought him equal parts of pleasure and
pain.

"Mmm-hmm," she said.

"It's early, but Celia's gonna be knocking on her feed bucket pretty soon."

"I'm used to early," she said.

"So what time do you get up for work, anyway?"

"Between two-thirty and three," she said.

"Good grief, you and Cleeve keep the same hours."

Olivia smiled, tipping her head back to study his face, even though she already knew every angle by heart, appreciating, nonetheless, the morning stubble on his jawline, the lazy sexiness in eyes that said the hours they had just spent together had not been nearly enough.

And they hadn't—they felt like just the tip of a beginning. And when he dipped forward to kiss her neck, she found herself wishing it would be just that. A beginning.

The sun broadened its hint, tiptoeing into the corners of the room, while they ignored the hour and enjoyed one another a while longer.

Voices sounded outside the office. John lifted his head and listened. "Sounds like Flora dragged Hank down to see if the baby was born last night."

"Daddy?" Flora called out.

"Go," Olivia said.

Leaving her was not his choice; his expression clearly said so. "Call me when you get back to the bed-and-breakfast?"

"I will," she said, her hand splayed on his chest,

his heart thudding against her palm. He did not want to leave her. And for now, it seemed like more than enough.

IT WAS ONE of those mornings when everything looks as if it's been rejuvenated overnight. The grass in the fields alongside the roads leading back to town was a brilliant green, still wet with dew. The sky was highlighted with trails of pink from the rising sun.

And Olivia felt the same rejuvenation within herself. A reawakening, an igniting of hope, and something else, too. Peace. The knowledge that she and John, after all these years, at least had that with one another. That, and that alone, filled places inside her that had been void, empty. She told herself not to be hopeful, not to attach too much meaning to what had happened between them last night.

But how could a woman not be hopeful when the man she had loved almost half her life had made love to her, the man whose hands made her feel as if she were some long-lost custom instrument that had finally been returned to its original and rightful owner?

How could she not be hopeful?

CHAPTER SIXTEEN

Second Chances

HANK HAD NEVER mentioned the fact that Olivia's car had been parked outside the barn that morning. And since there was no way he could have missed it, even if he'd walked by it with blinders on, John could only assume the older man was respecting his privacy.

For which he was grateful.

He'd stayed down at the barn with Flora for an hour or more. She could barely contain her excitement over the new foal, and he'd promised to bring her back a little later that morning after they'd given him time to rest.

He hurried through a shower, not wanting to miss Liv's call. How was it possible to feel like a seventeen-year-old again? A week ago, he would never have believed it possible of himself, and yet it was true. He felt as if he'd been injected with some life-altering wonder drug, and the future lay before him with a maze of possibilities that seemed staggering in their implication.

He pulled on jeans and boots, then stood in front of the sink and ran a razor over his face. His shower had steamed up the mirror above the sink. He erased the center with his palm and saw the differences in his face. Fog had finally lifted to let the sun in again. With that observation, something else settled in his chest. Fear. Outright terror, the roots going back a decade and a half. To have Liv again meant accepting the risk of losing her. Could he do that? Go forward without looking back? Without living in fear of having to learn how to live without her again?

He swiped the razor across one cheek, then reached over to crack open the window next to the sink. He set the blade to his face again, tilted his head and angled the razor down his jaw.

"Daddy!"

John looked out the window. His heart stopped, then bucked and raced off out of control.

"Daddy, look!"

Flora. On Naddie, loping bareback around the ring between the house and the barn.

He jerked the window up and stuck his head out. "Flora!" he called out, trying to keep the terror from his voice. "Just tug on the reins a little and ask her to stop."

"It's a surprise, Daddy!" she said. "See! I can ride Naddie!"

She couldn't hear him from there. Forcing himself

not to panic, John grabbed his shirt and bolted for the stairs, taking them two at a time.

At the bottom, he crossed the foyer in a couple of strides, yanked open the front door and hit the porch running. Halfway across the yard, he heard the ominous roar of a jet engine. His heart leapt to his throat. "Flora!" He waved, trying to get her attention. She was on the other side of the ring, her back to him. "Flora, get off! Baby, get off now!"

But the jet was already over the farm, its sudden roar sending Naddie into a terrified gallop around the ring.

John stopped, watched in paralyzed helplessness as Flora grabbed the filly's mane, the reins falling from her hands. She slid to the left, held on for a second longer and then dropped to the ground, her small head hitting the rock-dust footing first, her body limp like a broken doll's.

BACK AT LAVENDER HOUSE, Olivia took a shower and changed clothes, forcing herself to finish getting ready and pack her suitcase before calling John. She couldn't wait to hear his voice again. The need to see him hummed inside her like current through electrical wire.

Olivia. What have you done?

She was leaving this morning. So what happened now? What did they do now?

She had no answer. And maybe it was foolish to

ask. Maybe it was foolish to think there could be more than what they'd had in this weekend, which seemed so far removed from their normal lives.

But her heart paid no heed to the self-administered caution. She pulled the county phone book from the drawer beside the telephone, looked up the number, surprised to find that it was still the same and that she remembered it. She dialed, pulse thudding.

Sophia's brisk hello did not sound like Sophia at all.

"Sophia. It's Olivia," she said. "Is everything all right?"

"No. No, it's not," the older woman's voice cracked with emotion. "Flora's taken a bad fall off Naddie. We're waiting for the rescue squad."

All the air left Olivia's lungs. "Is she…is she going to be all right?"

"She's unconscious. We were afraid to move her. Oh, I hear it coming now."

"I'll meet you at the hospital, Sophia," Olivia said, fear making the words barely audible. She dropped the receiver, grabbed her things and raced from the room.

AMAZING HOW WORRY could siphon every other emotion from a person until the bones actually felt brittle with it. As if just to be touched would crumple any semblance of strength.

John sat beside his daughter in the ambulance as it tore down the county road toward town, its siren scream ominous, surreal. A paramedic put a stethoscope to Flora's chest for the second time since they'd left the farm. She had not yet regained consciousness. John stared down at her small form, fragile and vulnerable in a way that tore at his heart.

His daughter. His child.

How had this happened?

The answer came at him, obvious in its simplicity. And terrifying enough to roll him flat with a wave of defeat.

He could not protect the people he loved most in this life. Not Liv all those years ago when she'd been at the mercy of a father who had not deserved her. Not Laura with the awful illness that had drained the life from her. And now, not Flora.

He reached for her hand, squeezed it between his and prayed for God to hear his pleas.

OLIVIA HALF WALKED, half ran down the hospital corridor. At the registration desk, they directed her to the emergency room where she found Sophia and Hank, both looking as if they had aged ten years.

"Olivia," Sophia said, holding out her hand.

Olivia took it and then put her arms around the older woman, hugging her. "How is she?"

"We don't know yet. They're doing some kind

of X-ray, a cat scan, I think they said. John's with her.''

"She's going to be all right, Sophia. She just has to be."

They sat in the disinfectant-drenched waiting room an hour or more, the minutes crawling by, none of them willing to put voice to the worry etched in all their faces. At one point, Sophia, standing by the window with her arms wrapped around her waist, shook her head and said, "Dear heaven, if he loses that child…"

Olivia refused even to consider the possibility. Not Flora. Not that beautiful little girl. For John, for them all, Olivia could not bear the thought.

Finally, when every minute that passed had begun to feel like torture, a nurse came out and said, "Are you the Riley family?"

Olivia stepped back, but Sophia put a hand on her arm and said, "Yes, we are."

"Come with me," she said, and the set look on the young woman's mouth had Olivia imagining all the awful things they could be about to hear.

They followed her down a long hallway, the tile floor squeaking beneath their shoes.

"I'll wait out here," Olivia insisted when the nurse stopped in front of a room, the door half closed.

Sophia went inside while Olivia and Hank hovered at the entrance. Catching a glimpse of Flora's small form tucked into the white hospital bed, Olivia started to turn away, somehow feeling like an intruder. John looked up just then; their gazes caught and held, her heart twisting at the look in his eyes, proof that he had been through agony and then some since they'd left one another earlier that morning.

Sophia came out and beckoned them both in. "She's conscious," she said, a smile of pure relief on her lips.

John got up from the chair beside the bed and stepped toward Olivia, reservation on his face. "Thanks for coming," he said, distance in his voice.

Olivia felt suddenly unsure of her place here. "How is she?"

"She has a concussion. They want to keep her overnight for observation. But the doctor thinks she's going to be all right."

"Hi, Olivia and Hank," Flora said in a small voice that held no hint of the full-of-life child Olivia had spent time with that weekend.

Hank went to her, leaned down and planted an affectionate kiss on her forehead. "Hey, little bit. You gave us a good scare."

"I'm sorry, Hank."

Olivia took Flora's hand. "How are you feeling?"

"My head hurts."

"I had a concussion one time after I fell skiing. It made my head hurt, too," Olivia said.

"Did it hurt a long time?"

"Not too long."

"They've got some paperwork for me to fill out," John said, shoving his hands in the pockets of his jeans as if he didn't know what else to do with them.

"You go on," Sophia said.

He nodded once. "Be right back, sweet pea," he said to Flora and left the room.

Olivia felt the color drain from her face. John was understandably upset. But it was as if a wall had gone up around him. Maybe she shouldn't have come. Maybe it wasn't her place to be here. She looked up to find Sophia's gaze on hers, as if she understood something Olivia did not.

"Do I have to sleep in this all night, Sophia?" Flora asked, putting a hand on the standard-issue hospital gown.

"Not if I run home and get your pajamas. And how about Ace? That old teddy bear's not going to like sleeping in your bed without you."

"'Kay. Will you watch after Charlie while I'm gone?"

"She can stay in my room tonight." Sophia looked at Olivia. "Would you mind waiting here with her while Hank and I run back to the house?"

"Of course not," she said. And then, a shaft of uncertainty hitting her, "If you think John won't mind."

Sophia put a hand on her arm. "Be patient, dear,"

she said, her voice threaded with understanding. "If we're to have love in this life, we've got to be willing to face the pain of losing it. That's something he's going to have to accept sooner or later, unless he wants to miss out altogether."

Sophia's directness caught her off guard. Olivia had no idea how to respond, so she merely nodded.

"We should be back in a little while. I don't imagine John will be gone too long."

"We'll be fine," Olivia said.

Once Sophia and Hank had left, the room seemed too quiet.

"Do you feel all right?" Olivia asked the subdued child. "Is there anything I can get you? Some juice or water?"

Flora shook her head and fiddled with the edges of the bed sheet, her gaze on her hands. "I think I was way too bad this time. I knew Daddy didn't want me to ride Naddie."

Sensing there was more, Olivia waited.

"But if I'm not bad sometimes, maybe I'll have to leave like Mommy did."

"Oh, honey." Olivia's heart did a painful thump in her chest. She sat down on the chair beside the bed, took Flora's hands between her own, remembering then what the little girl had told her that first night from her raised window. Had that only been three days ago? It seemed as if a lifetime of events had happened since then. "I don't think your daddy ever meant for you to worry about that. I happen to believe that you were meant to be in your daddy's life. That there was a special purpose for it. And he loves you so much.''

"He's going to be mad at me for a really long time.''

Olivia squeezed the child's hands. "We all do things sometimes that we might not do again if we could rethink it. But that's part of growing and learning, and it's really nice when we get a second chance.''

"Will I get a second chance?''

"No doubt about it," Olivia said.

Movement turned her gaze to the door. John. The sight of him sent her heart galloping off in a confusion of gladness and uncertainty. The awkwardness between them now felt more like that of strangers than lovers.

"How's the patient?" he asked, his voice not quite steady.

"Good. Sophia and Hank ran back to the house to get a few things for her," Olivia said, feeling as if she needed to explain her presence and wondering how long he had been there.

John set a can of ginger ale and a cup of ice on the tray in front of Flora. "Thought you might be thirsty.''

"Thank you," Flora said, clearly subdued in her father's presence.

John crossed the floor to sit on the side of the bed, a finger tipping Flora's chin toward him. "I heard what you said to Liv just now. I never meant for you to think that being good meant you might have to leave me." He hesitated as if searching for words. "People say things sometimes when they're hurt or angry because they're struggling for a way to accept something that's happened to them. Your mama didn't die because she was a good woman. She was sick, and it was time for her not to suffer anymore. That's why she died. Do you understand that, honey?"

Flora nodded.

"And as for your worrying about me, it's my job to worry about you. That's what fathers do. Little girls aren't supposed to worry about their daddies or anything else." He reached out, pulled her into his arms and hugged her, the embrace full of love. "I'm not going anywhere, and you're not going anywhere."

Flora snuffled, wiped the back of her hand across her cheek where a tear had slipped past her long lashes. "Are you really mad at me, Daddy?"

"No," he said, "I'm not mad. But I had said it wasn't time for you to ride Naddie yet, so I think we're going to have to find some barn chores for you as punishment."

"Okay. Will they be hard?"

"Pretty hard," he said, making an obvious effort to look stern.

She considered that and then, "Olivia said I was meant to be in your life. That there was a special purpose for it."

"And that's the truth, baby." He pulled her to him again, hugging the child close.

Watching them, emotion knotted in Olivia's throat. Tears welled up and slipped down her cheeks. She felt that she did not belong here, that John's life was already carved out, that she was only kidding herself to think there might be a place for her in it.

And yet she did not have the courage to stay and see the proof in John's eyes that she was right.

She turned and quietly left the room.

CHAPTER SEVENTEEN

Fork in the Road

SHE WAS GONE.

And she hadn't said goodbye.

John had searched the hallway three times already end to end. No sign of her.

Damn.

In Flora's room, he went to the window with its view of Fourth and Main. He anchored a palm against the wall and stared at the cars driving by while something painful rolled through his chest.

He had no one to blame but himself. He'd been a perfect ass since he'd looked up to find her in the doorway. All he could think was, dear God, did he have the guts to love this woman again? Could he take care of her? Protect her as he had not been able to before?

What if he couldn't?

The door opened. He swung around, his heart leaping into his throat. It was Cleeve with an enormous stuffed gorilla tucked under one arm. "Hey," he said, disappointment sluicing through him even though he was glad Cleeve had come.

"Heard about the little rodeo queen," Cleeve said.

"She just fell asleep a few minutes ago."

Cleeve waved him out into the hall. "I don't wanna wake her up. Just wanted to make sure y'all were okay."

"She's going to be all right. Gave us a heck of a scare."

Cleeve shook his head, and John could see the relief on his friend's face. "I just passed Olivia pulling out of the parking lot. She was here, I take it?"

John sighed and looked his friend in the eye. "I think I blew it."

"You plannin' on doing anything about it?"

John shoved a hand through his hair and acknowledged his own uncertainty. "What if it doesn't work out between us?"

"What if it does?" Cleeve set the gorilla down on the floor beside him, the banana in its hand flopping to the side. "Macy's been having an affair."

The admission caught John like a right hook to the jaw. "Ah, hell, Cleeve."

The wattage in Cleeve's smile looked as if it took effort. "Thought I'd make up one of those signs—Woman Wanted. Must Have Good Tractor. Please Send Photo of Tractor."

It was just like Cleeve to throw a piece of life-changing information out with a wall of humor in front of it for protection. But John had known him a long time, and he heard the seam of pain running through the words. "I'm sorry."

"Three strikes, and you're supposed to be out, huh?"

"Those are somebody else's rules," John said. "I'm beginning to wonder if the game's not played a little better when we don't try so hard to act like we have the whole thing figured out. I don't have any of it figured out, Cleeve. All I know is I love Liv, that I don't guess I ever stopped loving her, and I've never been more scared of anything in my life."

"So back to my original question. What if it does work out between you? Be pretty great, huh?"

"Yeah. Pretty great."

"I guess it's like those cliffs out at the lake we used to dive off in the summertime. It was a lot safer standing on that ledge watching everybody else take the plunge. But it was a hell of a lot of fun jumping in."

John nodded, smiling.

"So. Looks like we've both had a little epiphany this weekend."

"Big word for a cowboy."

"I'll get you a dictionary."

It was as close as the two of them ever got to a heart to heart. But there was one thing John could not deny. This weekend had led them both to a fork in the road. Cleeve had decided the direction he intended to take. Now John had to do the same.

IT WASN'T AS IF she hadn't known the risk.

She'd driven out to that barn last night with her eyes wide open and had known exactly what was at stake. She and John were adults, and they hadn't made each other any promises.

The Summerville Town Limits sign was just ahead on the right. Olivia had promised Lori she would come by on her way out of town. She had to hold it together until then. She had a four-hour drive ahead of her. There would be plenty of time for playing what-ifs. Like the rest of her life. So she turned the radio up extra loud. Kept her window rolled down and the sunroof open.

But the music was no dam for the tears in her eyes or the ache in her heart.

Something flashed in her rearview mirror.

She looked up. John's truck. A simultaneous rush of hope and gladness anchored itself in the center of her chest. The mind could throw out rational, it's-for-the-best placards all day long, but the heart had its own agenda, said what it wanted to say.

He flicked his lights.

She eased the car into the gravel parking lot of Atner's Country Store.

He had gotten out of the truck. She lowered the

window, schooled her features into neutrality and hoped her eyes weren't as tear-swollen as they felt.

He stopped beside her door, looked down at her with eyes that were serious, and something else, too. Humble?

"Liv, we can't leave things like this," he said.

"You shouldn't have come. You need to be with Flora."

"Sophia is with her. She's fine. Will you leave your car here for a little while and come with me?"

She should have said no then and there. That would have been the safe thing to do, the logical thing. But aware of that as she was, she nodded once, pulled the car into one of the store's parking spaces and got out. She didn't want to expect anything. Didn't want to *want* anything. But logic stood no chance against a heart that had yearned as many years as hers had.

Inside the truck, the silence between them was uncertain, full of questions that felt as if they could never possibly have an answer. They drove a couple of miles before John flipped the blinker and turned onto a dirt road that edged alongside a field of boot-high grass.

"I bought this land a few years ago for cutting hay," he said. "All right if we sit out here?"

Again, she nodded, not ready yet to trust her voice enough for words.

A quarter mile or so off the main road, he

stopped, cut the engine, and they got out. John sat down on the front bumper and patted the spot beside him.

Olivia sat, crossed her legs, then her hands on her lap. Put voice, finally, to the words she should have said back at the country store. "Don't you think it would be simpler if we just filed this weekend away as something unexpected and went on with our lives? What happened last night wasn't a promise of anything, John. I know that."

Her words hung there between them for what felt like too long, stretched beyond their shape like a wet sweater hung on a line to dry.

"Liv." He turned, angled a leg so that it touched hers. He reached out and traced a finger along the line of her jaw, a caress of wordless disagreement. "For me, it couldn't have been anything other than that."

"John—"

But he didn't let her finish, going on as if he had something to say that needed to be said. "I don't know if I can even explain in words what having you here again has done to me. It's like it was when I loved you before. I'll never be the same person again."

Olivia blinked. Tears welled up, blurring her vision.

He laid his hand on top of hers, turned it over and entwined his fingers with hers, squeezing them tight.

"This morning when I saw Flora lying on the ground like that, I thought I might lose her. It felt like all the blood drained out of me. That without her, I would turn to dust and just blow away. That's what it's like to love someone that much. It's not a choice. It's like breathing. That's how I love you, Liv. As if without you, I might stop breathing altogether. But it seems like I haven't been able to protect the people I love most in this world, to keep bad things from happening to them."

The words fell across Olivia, and the sincerity of them, the vulnerability of them, the recognition of the deep place from which they came, brought fresh tears to her eyes. She understood now Sophia's quiet urging from earlier. *If we're to have love in this life, we've got to be willing to face the pain of losing it.*

This, then, was John's fear. And Olivia understood it. Maybe it *would* be easier to walk away, not to give themselves a chance at a future. But then how would they ever know? And what precious things might they lose?

She pressed the palm of her hand to his cheek. "If I start my life again without you, it's going to feel like a shell with nothing worthwhile on the inside."

He put his arms around her, folded her into him and dipped his head into the curve of her neck. She felt his heartbeat, hard and insistent, felt, too, the force of emotion behind it.

They held each other for a long time. Moments of healing, of new beginnings. Olivia felt it in the farthest reaches of her own heart.

She leaned back, brushed her hand across his cheek. He had become the man promised in the boy she had loved long ago. And she loved him now as she had then, with every breath. "There aren't any guarantees in this life, for any of us. We just love as long as we can, the best that we can. The very best that we can."

He stood, took her hand and pulled her close, so that her feet barely stayed on the ground. And he kissed her, long and full, the kiss of a man claiming a woman as his own, accepting the risk and consequences of doing so. And it was what Olivia wanted to be. His. For the rest of her life. For the rest of his.

They kissed for a good long while, took their time with it like two people with the right to do so. John pulled back finally, one hand cupping the side of her neck. "So how's a city girl like you going to work out a life with a country boy like me?" The question had lightness at the edges, but concern at its core.

"Didn't you know I've always had a thing for country boys? You see, I met one a long time ago. And I never got over him."

"Hmm," John said, smiling now. "Should I be jealous?"

"He's a tough act to follow."

"I'll give it my best shot."

"What more could a girl ask?" And then, glancing down, searching for words, she said, "Maybe it won't be simple at first, but I want room for this, for us."

"Then let's start with that," he said, drawing her to him again. "I love you. If we let that be the center, the rest will work out around it."

How simple the words, and yet within their structure, a lifetime of meaning, past, present, future.

"Can you stay tonight?"

"I don't have to be back until Tuesday morning," she said. "Let's go check on Flora. And then I'd like to see Lori. There are a few things I need to explain."

John kissed her again then, under the shady boughs of an old elm tree. And there they began their life together, two paths separate for so long now merged as one.

EPILOGUE

THE WEDDING took place on a Sunday at Rolling Hills Farm. The guest list was small, each person there someone who really mattered to the man and woman committing themselves to one another this bright September day.

Happiness filled the air, tangible and real.

The two people standing side by side in front of the preacher were happy, the kind of happy that comes from the complete giving of oneself to another human being, and that person's willing acceptance of that gift. It was there on their faces, easy to read.

The little girl with the long ponytail stood next to them with a huge bouquet of white azaleas in her small hands. And she was smiling.

The best man had a big grin on his face; every minute or two he would throw a glance over his shoulder at the pretty, dark-haired woman sitting in the front row. And every time he did, her eyes were on him, and he felt like a schoolboy in love for the first time.

The matron of honor had already gone through

three hankies, but the tears sliding down her face met up with the smile on her lips and melted away.

There in the front yard, a huge old oak tree cast fingers of shade across the wedding party. The dog sitting beneath it thumped its tail against the grass.

The sun shone down on the gathering, not too hot, Indian summer all the old-timers around called it. The sky was clear, so clear that from where they stood, the two people vowing to love one another for the rest of their lives could see all the way to the rolling hills at the back of the farm, and beyond if they looked hard enough.

*   *   *   *   *

*Watch for Inglath Cooper's next
Superromance novel, coming in July 2004.
Available wherever Harlequin
books are sold.*

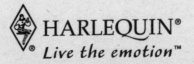

If you enjoyed what you just read,
then we've got an offer you can't resist!

Take 2 bestselling love stories FREE!

Plus get a FREE surprise gift!

Clip this page and mail it to Harlequin Reader Service®

IN U.S.A.	IN CANADA
3010 Walden Ave.	P.O. Box 609
P.O. Box 1867	Fort Erie, Ontario
Buffalo, N.Y. 14240-1867	L2A 5X3

YES! Please send me 2 free Harlequin Superromance® novels and my free surprise gift. After receiving them, if I don't wish to receive anymore, I can return the shipping statement marked cancel. If I don't cancel, I will receive 6 brand-new novels every month, before they're available in stores. In the U.S.A., bill me at the bargain price of $4.47 plus 25¢ shipping and handling per book and applicable sales tax, if any*. In Canada, bill me at the bargain price of $4.99 plus 25¢ shipping and handling per book and applicable taxes**. That's the complete price, and a savings of at least 10% off the cover prices—what a great deal! I understand that accepting the 2 free books and gift places me under no obligation ever to buy any books. I can always return a shipment and cancel at any time. Even if I never buy another book from Harlequin, the 2 free books and gift are mine to keep forever.

135 HDN DNT3
336 HDN DNT4

Name	(PLEASE PRINT)	
Address	Apt.#	
City	State/Prov.	Zip/Postal Code

* Terms and prices subject to change without notice. Sales tax applicable in N.Y.
** Canadian residents will be charged applicable provincial taxes and GST.
   All orders subject to approval. Offer limited to one per household and not valid to current Harlequin Superromance® subscribers.
   ® is a registered trademark of Harlequin Enterprises Limited.

SUP02   ©1998 Harlequin Enterprises Limited

Ordinary people.
Extraordinary circumstances.

CODE RED

Meet the dedicated emergency service workers of Courage Bay, California. They're always ready to answer the call.

Father by Choice
by M.J. Rodgers
(Harlequin Superromance
#1194 April 2004)

Silent Witness
by Kay David
(Harlequin Superromance
#1200 May 2004)

The Unknown Twin
by Kathryn Shay
(Harlequin Superromance
#1206 June 2004)

And be sure to watch for *Heatwave*,
a Code Red single title anthology coming in July 2004.

Available wherever Harlequin Books are sold.

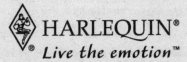

HARLEQUIN®
Live the emotion™

Visit us at www.eHarlequin.com   HSRCODER